MIRROR MIRROR

Mirror Mirror: The Movie Novel

Based on Relativity's Motion Picture

Adapted by Lexi Ryals

Based upon the screenplay by Melisa Wallack and Jason Keller

Based on the Grimm Brothers' "Little Snow White"

Directed by Tarsem Singh

SCHOLASTIC INC.

New York   Toronto   London   Auckland
Sydney   Mexico City   New Delhi   Hong Kong

ISBN 978-0-545-43675-5

12 11 10 9 8 7 6 5 4 3 2 1   12 13 14 15 16 17/0

Printed in the U.S.A.   40
First printing, January 2012

prologue: a note from the queen

Once upon a time, in a kingdom long ago, a baby girl was born. Her hair was the color of night, her skin was pure as snow . . . she was, essentially, the most overrated baby in all the land.

They called her Snow White (probably because that was the most pretentious name they could come up with). As fate would have it, her mother died in childbirth. But don't feel sad for dear Snow—you see, her father was the king. He loved Snow. Spoiled her. Lavished every minute on the wretched little girl.

The King raised his daughter by himself. He was grooming

her to lead one day. He took her on rides to visit his loyal subjects in the disgustingly happy nearby village. He taught her how to spar. He read her bedtime stories and tucked her in at night.

But over time, the King realized there were some things he couldn't teach her — things like how to style her hair or how to be a lady — things that needed a woman's touch. So he looked far and wide for a new queen to help him raise Snow.

That's where I make my grand entrance.

The King was bewitched by me. And who wouldn't be? I was the most beautiful woman in the land, and, just to clarify, "most beautiful woman in the land" isn't hyperbole; I was literally given the title. Of course the little love potion I slipped into his drink didn't hurt either.

But even my magic didn't stand a chance against Snow White. He would never love me more than that little brat, and if I couldn't have his whole heart, then she couldn't either. Before the King went hunting one day, I gave him a magic half-moon pendant that matched my own. With it around his neck, I controlled the King almost completely, not that he knew that then. It just seemed like a sweet present from his new bride. But did he give me a gift in return? No! Instead he gave Snow White a gift — a beautifully polished golden dagger.

That was the last gift he would ever give his precious Snow White — or anyone else. Tragedy struck on that hunting trip.

The King's horse returned alone and the King was never seen again. A horrific beast had invaded the dark forest and that beast was the end of the King. Snow was left alone to be raised by me, the Queen.

As time passed, Snow White grew older. And I realized something: If I wanted to remain the most beautiful woman in the land . . . well, Snow would have to do what snow does best. . . .

Snow would have to fall.

As for what happened next, I'll let you judge for yourself. But if you choose the wrong side, don't say I didn't warn you. It never pays to mess with me.

—The Queen

chapter one

Snow White leaned on the ledge of her bedroom window and sighed, her crimson lips bent in a frown. Her dark hair shined in the late-afternoon sunlight as she let her blue eyes study the snow-covered forest below her tower. She was half hoping that someone would ride out of the woods to take her far, far away from the castle and her stepmother—not that it would ever happen. She didn't even know anyone outside of the castle and she knew the Queen did her best to make sure no one even remembered Snow White existed. It was obviously working. After all, it was her eighteenth birthday and not a single person had remembered.

Why would anyone remember or even care that it's my birthday? she thought sadly.

4

Just then, a little bird flew up and landed on the ledge and twittered a greeting.

"Oh, hello there!" Snow White smiled sweetly. "Would you like a treat?" She picked up a piece of apple from her lunch plate and placed it in front of the bird. He ate greedily, stopping only when a noise from below startled him.

"That's just the guests arriving for the Queen's party," Snow assured him.

He tilted his little head and chirped a question at her, before going back to eating.

"No, I'm not going to the party. I'm definitely not allowed. You have a better chance of being invited to that party than I do," she replied.

The little bird finished eating, twittered a good-bye, and then flew away.

"Eat and run. That's so easy for you. . . ." Snow stared after him wistfully.

Maybe I could go down for a little while, she thought. *It is my birthday. . . . Maybe the Queen won't mind.*

Before she could lose her nerve, Snow smoothed her plain dress and slipped out the door.

chapter two

The Queen was having one of her famous parties, but she wasn't enjoying it very much. All of the lords and ladies of the land were helping her play a new game she had devised to help pass another snowy winter afternoon. The Queen was facing off against a wealthy baron. They each had a team of players standing on a large board of numbered and lettered tiles. All of the people on the board were wearing hats in the shape of boats with miniature cannons attached to them. The guests were having the time of their lives—but the Queen was bored.

"F to D9," the Queen said lazily, twisting one of her coppery curls around her perfectly manicured finger.

Lord Waverly, a short, stout man wearing a tugboat on

his bald head, nodded and stepped forward tentatively.

"To your left, Lord Waverly," the Queen corrected.

The poor man looked around nervously before taking a small step to his right. The Queen closed her eyes and massaged the spot between her eyes to ward off a headache caused by the lord's complete incompetence.

"If someone would please teach Lord Waverly his right from his left, I'd be so very grateful," she instructed. A lady wearing a yacht hat shoved the lost lord to the left. "Thank you."

"F to D9. A brilliant move, Your Majesty," the Queen's opponent, the Baron, said.

"Yes, well, it's Lord Waverly who makes it all seem so effortless," she replied without looking up.

"And dare I say, you look absolutely radiant today," the Baron continued. The Queen finally smiled. She loved being complimented on her looks. It was the only thing she never got tired of.

"You may 'dare say,' Baron. You may always 'dare say' such things," she smiled and then lifted a silver goblet so she could check her reflection in its shiny side. Even distorted in the goblet, her reflection was beautiful.

"B to J12," the Baron called out before leaning in to whisper to the Queen. "I feel it's my duty to tell you . . . of rumors I've been hearing."

7

"Rumors? What do you mean, 'rumors'?" the Queen replied, setting the goblet down.

"Just idle chatter."

"I detest idle chatter."

"Don't we all! Yet there is little we can do about it," the Baron continued suggestively.

"Men without tongues don't tend to chatter. So there's an option," the Queen replied coldly before flashing the Baron a tight smile. "F to C6!" She shouted while he laughed nervously. "I could keep up our witty repartee all day, alas, I've a kingdom to run. So cut to it. What have you heard?"

"Well, there have been rumblings among the Nobility. A few have said . . . that the kingdom may be close to destitute."

The Queen's eyes narrowed down to slits for a split second before she hid her fury behind a dazzling smile. She held up her hand to stop the Baron from speaking again.

"Brighton? A word, please?" the Queen called out sweetly to a servant standing a few feet away.

Brighton, a short, nervous, middle-aged man and the Queen's favorite minion, rushed over to the throne.

"Your Majesty?" he answered.

"Loose lips sink ships," the Queen practically purred.

"Yes, Your Majesty! Exactly! Which ship would you like

sunk?" He gestured at the human boats on the game board below.

"It's an expression, Brighton," the Queen explained slowly, as she would to a small child. "It's also a new Royal Decree. Take it down."

"Ah, marvelous!" Brighton whipped out a scroll and a feather quill, still blushing under the Queen's haughty gaze.

"Any busybodies caught rumoring, gossiping, or speculating—"

"How about 'scuttlebutting'?" Brighton interrupted.

"'Scuttlebutting'?" she scoffed. "You always overshoot."

"Er. Uh, 'whispering'?"

"Certainly. Anyone caught whispering, or even thinking . . . shall be put to death." She paused. "How does that sound?"

"It's decisive," he confirmed, scribbling away.

The Queen and her guests were so focused on the Queen's new decree that no one noticed Snow White slip into the room and hide behind a pillar.

"B to F7!" the Baron shouted before turning his attention back to the Queen. "Let me be frank. It's no secret that the kingdom is in ruins."

"Ruins?" The Queen arched one thin eyebrow.

"My lady, as you know, I've been looking for a bride," the

Baron continued, seemingly oblivious to the fact that he was on thin ice with the Queen already. "Were we to join our two houses, I think the gentry would feel reassured that the kingdom was stable once again."

"Marry you?" The Queen looked utterly disgusted at the idea, but quickly hid it with a smile.

"It's just an inkling of an idea. You would make a beautiful bride."

"Oh, Baron, I'm flattered at the notion. But as you know, I'm still in mourning," the Queen answered smoothly.

"It's been years."

"These things take time," she said, looking around for an exit from the conversation. Suddenly, her eyes flashed with anger as she spotted Snow White watching the party from behind an elegantly carved pillar. "Snow White, do you think I'm blind?"

The Queen beckoned her forward to the throne. "Is there a fire?"

"I'm sorry?" Snow asked, glancing around quickly to see if there was indeed a fire.

"In your bedroom? Is your bedroom on fire? Because I'm searching for an explanation as to why you'd be out of your bedroom and in here. My first guess was fire."

"Well, I thought maybe . . . I could come to the gala. You

know, because today is . . . my eighteenth birthday," Snow answered meekly.

"Is it now? My, oh my. Time sure has flown." The Queen turned back to the board. "E to F3, please. Thank you."

The Queen focused her attention back on Snow White and looked her up and down critically before speaking again, quietly, so that no one but the two of them could hear. "Maybe it's time I ease up on you, Snow White. After all, you've done nothing to me. You do as I say. You cause no problems. But, yet, there is something about you that is just so incredibly irritating. I don't know what it is—the slumped shoulders, or the hair, or the voice. You know what, I think it's the hair. I hate your hair."

Snow White winced with each word, her bottom lip trembling with the effort to keep from crying. The Queen leaned forward. She was enjoying every bit of pain on Snow's face. "Let me tell you a secret. A leader's greatest gift is that they can look into someone's eyes and know exactly what they are. And I look into your eyes and, it makes no rational sense, I know, but I hate you. And I don't care if it's your one hundredth birthday—don't you dare ever sneak into a party like this again."

"F to E6," the Baron called out, oblivious to the conversation he was interrupting.

"C to D4," the Queen answered without even looking at

the board. "Baron, you've been beaten and you don't even know it. . . ."

The Baron's eyes scanned the board frantically, looking for an escape.

"Come now, Baron. Acknowledging and accepting defeat is an essential part of life. Isn't that true, Snow White?"

Snow White's gaze dropped to the ground. She should have just given up. What had she been thinking sneaking down to the party?

The Baron's gaze dropped, too. He spotted his mistake. He bowed stiffly to the Queen, conceding his loss. With that, one of the Queen's players shot his miniature cannon at one of the Baron's players, ending the game with a boom. As smoke filled the air and the lords and ladies rushed to congratulate the Queen, Snow slipped away toward the kitchens, wiping tears from her eyes.

chapter three

Snow White paused for a moment in the hallway to compose herself before walking into the kitchen to find some dinner. She dried one last tear on the hem of her sleeve and then pushed open the heavy wooden door.

"Happy birthday, Snow!"

The entire kitchen staff had been waiting for her. They even had a large cupcake with a candle for her to blow out. Snow White was completely surprised and touched by their thoughtfulness.

"You remembered. . . !" She exclaimed.

After Snow thanked everyone, Baker Margaret pulled her aside. Margaret was the closest thing Snow had ever had to a mother. She was thankful Margaret had remained working for the Queen for so many years—not everyone had.

"Thank you so much," Snow said, giving the older woman a hug.

"Of course! A girl's eighteenth birthday is the most important of them all. Close your eyes, make a wish, and may it come true," Margaret instructed.

Without hesitating, Snow said, "I wish for the kingdom and all its people to prosper." She bent forward, ready to blow out the candle, but Margaret reached out and covered Snow's mouth.

"Oh, for heaven's sake, you only turn eighteen once, Snow. Surely you're allowed *one* measly wish for yourself."

"No. Thank you, Margaret, but no," Snow answered, shaking her head. She couldn't allow herself to think that way.

"Would you like to know *my* wish, then, Snow White?"

"You can't make a wish for me. . . ."

"Do you know why I've continued working for that wretched Queen for so many years?" Margaret interrupted, pulling a wrapped gift from her apron pocket and handing it to a surprised Snow. "It's not because I want to watch over you—though I do. It's not even because I love you—though that's true as well. I do it because I believe that one day you will take back your kingdom. And I want to be here when that happens. I want to be here when *you* start to believe."

14

Snow White hung her head sadly. "It is not my kingdom."

"Oh, but it is. Your father meant for you to inherit his crown. And instead, that wretched woman has the entire kingdom convinced that you're a pathetic shut-in, incapable of leaving the castle. And the worst part is, she has you believing it. Now open your present."

Trembling a bit, Snow White tore the paper off of the box and opened it to find her gold dagger, polished and looking as lovely as it did the day her father gave it to her so many years ago. She thought she had lost it the day her father's horse came back alone. She had been practicing with the dagger on a bale of hay when she saw the horse. She'd run into the forest to look for her dad and she kept running until one of the guards caught her and carried her back.

"Oh!" Snow exclaimed. Just looking at the dagger reminded her of her father. She missed him more than ever.

"I found it buried in a drawer. Had it cleaned and polished."

"That was very kind of you. But what would I do with this?"

"I can think of one thing off the top of my head," Margaret answered, tilting her head in the direction of the throne room where the Queen was holding court. Snow White looked horrified. "You could take her down. But if that's too drastic . . . perhaps it's at least time you see for yourself what goes on in your kingdom. I see so much of your father in you, Snow. You are the kindest and the fairest young woman I've ever known. So my wish for you, Snow White, is this: I wish for you to show the world those qualities. And if the world's too big, I wish for you to show them to yourself."

Then Margaret blew the candle out.

chapter four

The next day, a handsome young prince from a neighboring kingdom, and his valet, Renbock, entered the dark and shadowy woods around Snow White's kingdom.

"I certainly don't like the woods, sire. If you don't mind me saying, they seem a bit . . . sinister," Renbock said to the Prince, his voice echoing loudly in the silence.

"They're only trees, Renbock. And trees are only wood."

"There are stories of a man-eating beast inhabiting these parts."

"Nonsense. Children's tales," the Prince answered, but he sped up his pace, eager to find the Beast. The Prince had been searching for a proper adventure for months—after all, he

17

needed to prove himself worthy as a prince with some heroic deed. Slaying a man-eating beast would be perfect.

Renbock pulled out a map and a compass from his saddlebag and spread it out on his lap. "If you don't mind me asking, when does Your Highness think we will be heading home? We've been on the road for months—perhaps we could head down to the coast? It's so terribly cold and snowy here. Maybe someplace a bit more balmy . . ."

"A man doesn't prove himself by sailing, Renbock! He proves himself by placing his body in harm's way! Battle! That is what I seek. . . ."

The prince stopped midsentence as a mixture of strange noises drifted toward them through the trees. The banging and clomping grew closer and closer.

"It must be the Beast!" the Prince exclaimed. He halted his horse, eagerly dismounted, and pulled out his sword, ready to do battle.

The clomping grew louder until it reached a thunderous pitch as seven giants, towering over them at nearly eight feet tall, emerged from the trees.

"Giants!" the Prince shouted. "That's almost as good as a beast!"

"This is crazy!" Renbock exclaimed, turning his horse to ride away, but a giant blocked his way.

"Empty your pockets! This is a robbery," one of the giants shouted.

"Never!" shouted the Prince, hopping over a snowdrift to jab the first giant with his sword.

With that, each of the giants pulled out dangerously sharp–looking swords. The Prince whirled and jabbed, battling them all! Renbock stayed on his horse and cheered from the sidelines. The Prince was very good with his sword and was starting to push the giants back. But suddenly, the giants started hopping and flipping around too quickly for the Prince to keep up. It was strange — giants generally did not have a reputation for being agile.

The Prince fought frantically, but he was almost over-whelmed. A giant pinned him against a tree, but he kept struggling. He finally got his leg free and kicked the giant's legs. With a sickening crack, the giant's legs snapped and he fell to the ground. In the process, he lost his boots and half of his height. The giant stood up in a daze. He only stood four feet tall.

It took a moment for the Prince and Renbock to realize that he wasn't a giant! They were fighting dwarves on stilts.

"You're . . . you're a dwarf!" Renbock gasped and began to giggle. The Prince joined him and soon they were both laughing so hard that they fell to the ground, clutching their stomachs and trying to catch their breath.

"Stand up and fight!" the dwarf demanded.

"You can't expect me to fight you," the Prince finally said between chuckles.

"Why not!" another dwarf named Grimm demanded.

"Because he's a shrimp. As are you. It wouldn't be sporting," the Prince replied.

"'Shrimp'! That's the best you got?" a dwarf named Napoleon snarled, slashing forward with his sword and forcing the Prince to defend himself.

"So uninspired," Grimm, the clear leader of the group, agreed, stepping in to fight the Prince as Napoleon stepped back.

"Worse than 'shorty,'" a dwarf named Chuck replaced Grimm.

"'Fun-sized,'" Wolf, a fierce-looking dwarf spun in to join Chuck.

"'Niblet,'" a chubby dwarf named Grub added, jumping in.

"No matter how you describe it, you are all short!" the Prince replied, fighting fiercely and looking a little nervous. He tripped and stumbled to the ground. "And that is funny. . . ."

The dwarf named Butcher shoved his gleaming knife against the Prince's throat. "Not as funny as what my knife's gonna do to your royal neck."

The Prince gulped, trying to pull away from the blade.

Grimm stepped forward and tapped Butcher on the shoulder. "Take it easy, all we want is his gold. We're not murderers. Anything worth taking?"

The tiniest dwarf in the group, Half-Pint, strode over to the horses and rummaged through the Prince's bags. "I got his saddlebag!" he exclaimed just as he tripped over a tree root. The saddlebag sailed through the air and hit the ground, spilling gold and other treasure all over the forest floor.

The dwarves all raced to pick up the spilled treasure. One dwarf counted the coins and another began munching on the Prince's leftover turkey leg from lunch.

"Hey! That's my lunch!" the Prince said, getting up and dusting himself off. "This is absurd! I will fight you to the death before I let you dishonor me this way."

"Sire, just give them what they want," Renbock hissed quietly. He had ducked behind the snowy branches of a large bush, hoping the dwarves might forget about him altogether if he didn't draw any attention to himself.

"Nonsense. I intend to teach these children a lesson," the Prince declared haughtily.

Suddenly, all the Dwarves spun and glared at the Prince, livid.

"'Children'?" Grimm asked, his eyes narrowed in anger.

They raised their blades. The Prince's eyes widened. He

realized his mistake as the dwarves rose back up on their stilts.

Five minutes later, the dwarves were gone, and the Prince and Renbock were hog-tied and dangling upside down from a tree in their underwear. The day couldn't possibly have gotten any worse.

"How embarrassing. I can't believe we were robbed by dwarves," Renbock sighed.

"Nobody needs to know the details, Renbock. Understood?" the Prince answered grimly.

If word got out that the Prince had been defeated by a pack of dwarves, he would never live it down. He was going to have to do something about those tiny bandits if he ever wanted to prove himself and salvage his reputation. But first, they needed help!

chapter five

The Queen needed some help herself. She was rapidly running out of money and she needed a way to get rid of the Baron intent on marrying her. She knew he wasn't going to give up unless she could prove that the kingdom was alright financially. Too bad the Royal Treasury was down to its last few coins. She only had one option left.

She snuck away from the great hall and locked herself in her private chamber, a lavish room dominated by a full-length mirror surrounded by an intricate gilded frame.

The Queen stood in front of the mirror and reached out one slender hand to touch its surface. "Mirror, mirror, on the wall. Reveal the truth, thou knowest all. . . ."

As she spoke, the mirror grew brighter and brighter until it shone with a pure white light. Then the Queen stepped forward and disappeared through the shining glass.

The Queen emerged on the other side of the mirror in a strange garden on a path leading to a charming cottage. She dusted off her hands and walked quickly to the cottage and stepped inside. A mirror identical to the one from the palace hung on the wall.

The Queen stood in front of it and stared at her reflection. She saw a truly beautiful woman—with coppery, shining hair, smooth soft skin, and sharp, intelligent brown eyes above chiseled cheekbones. But the Mirror Queen was not a reflection at all; she was the magic the Queen carried deep inside of her—her alter ego.

"Can you believe that Baron? I mean, honestly, did he really think I'd consider marrying him?" The Queen sighed to the Mirror Queen, wrinkling her nose while the Mirror Queen remained still. "A woman has standards, after all. And an exalted woman like myself has very high standards. . . ."

"Interesting," the Mirror Queen finally replied in a bored tone.

"What is?"

"Your response to his proposal."

"What is that supposed to mean?" the Queen demanded.

"It means the clock is ticking."

"On what?"

"On everything. On your looks. Your treasury. Our magic. Like everything else, they all come to an end. Consider the options," the Mirror Queen replied in the same nasty tone the Queen herself usually reserved only for Snow White.

"This option has a receding hairline and smells like rotten eggs and I wouldn't be caught dead with him!" the Queen exclaimed, her voice dripping with disgust.

"You can't afford to say no! You've spent so much supporting your vanity."

"Well, then," the Queen snapped. "Why don't you just snap your fingers and make me a chest of gold?"

"Everyone has magic within them, but very few discover it and learn to spend it wisely," the Mirror Queen explained. "You already know that. Yet you have used so much of your magic already. You do not want to spend what's left on a bit of gold. You will one day pay a great price for trivial purchases. Trust me."

"Well, what do you suggest I do?"

"I suggest you marry someone rich. Quickly. Because one day soon you're going to ask me who the fairest of them all is. And you're not going to like the answer," the Mirror Queen promised, her voice as cold as ice.

chapter six

That same morning, Snow White took a deep breath before opening her door and tiptoeing down the hallway in her thick cloak. She almost turned back when she saw a palace guard walking toward her, but instead she squared her shoulders, shook back her hair, and kept walking.

"Good evening, Princess," he said politely.

"Good evening. I'm going . . . out," Snow answered, surprised at how confident she sounded.

Before the guard could stop her, Snow hurried on down the hall and slipped out a side door that led into the dark and snowy forest. She was free.

After walking for quite a ways, Snow wasn't feeling as confident as she had been when she left. The woods were cold, wet, dark, and full of strange noises that made her feel jumpy.

Maybe I should just go back, she thought to herself. Just then a loud noise echoed through the trees.

"This is crazy. I can't do this," she whispered, fear making her voice catch in her throat.

She began to turn around when she heard the noise again, but this time she could make out words.

"Help! Someone!"

She couldn't just leave—not if one of her subjects needed her help. So Snow took a deep breath and followed the sound down the path, her dagger out and ready, just in case.

"Is anyone out there? Please!"

The voice was so clear that Snow knew she was close. She pushed aside some heavy branches and walked into a small clearing where the Prince and Renbock were hanging from a tree in their underwear.

Her mouth dropped open. This was not at all what she had been expecting to find. Then, unable to control herself, she began to laugh.

"I was warned of what I might find in the woods . . . but I never imagined this," she managed to say in greeting between giggles.

The Prince twisted around, swinging from his ankles and trying to get a look at her.

"Who laughs at me? Reveal yourself!" he demanded.

Snow stepped forward into a shaft of dappled sunlight right in front of the Prince and pushed back her hood. His eyes widened. She was beautiful—even upside down.

"We are in dire need of your help, ma'am," Renbock explained. "We were ambushed by seven dwar—"

"—bloodthirsty giants!" The Prince interrupted, embarrassed to let such a lovely girl know he had been bested by dwarves.

"Giants?" Snow repeated.

"They were quite vicious. We fought a brave battle, but alas, we were outnumbered," the Prince continued.

"Young lady, if you would be so kind as to help me and the honorable Prince of—" Renbock began.

"Prince of nothing! Stop babbling, you fool!" the Prince exclaimed, cutting Renbock off. "I am but a . . . commoner in need of a helping hand. Now then, I order you to cut us down this instant."

"You order me?" Snow replied, raising an eyebrow at him quizzically.

"Refuse and you shall suffer dire consequences," the Prince finished.

"You could at least say 'please,'" Snow replied sweetly.

"Given the circumstances, sir, I think a 'please' is in order," Renbock hissed at the Prince, swinging as close to him as possible.

The Prince blushed. "Of course. Where are my manners? Please."

With that, Snow White reached up and awkwardly used her golden dagger to slice through the ropes holding the two up.

The men tumbled immediately to the ground, landing with a thud in a heap with the Prince's face against Renbock's behind.

"Ugh," the Prince groaned, pushing Renbock off of him and standing up with as much dignity as he could muster. He turned, brushing the snow off of himself, and faced Snow. She was even more beautiful right side up.

"Oh!" Snow White gave a startled gasp as she finally got a clear look at the Prince. He was so handsome. Even in his underwear, he seemed confident.

"I apologize, young lady. You stand before a man who just had his face up his friend's rump," the Prince said sheepishly.

"Your face seems no worse for wear," Snow replied with a smile. The Prince grinned back at her. "Although you might consider getting dressed before you catch frostbite."

"Thank you for your help. We are . . . traveling south," the Prince said hopefully.

"Ah. I am traveling . . . north."

"That's a shame," the Prince replied.

"Yes. It is," she said with a small sigh, sad to see him go.

The Prince bowed graciously and kissed her hand. "Then, I bid you farewell." He and Rencok turned and started toward the palace.

Snow stared at her hand, where the Prince had just kissed it. Then she smiled as she turned toward the village. She wondered if she would ever see him again.

Snow looked back over her shoulder, only to find the Prince staring back at her over his shoulder with a grin on his face. She smiled and blushed, and then pushed through the trees, out of sight.

Renbock and the Prince walked up the path until they caught sight of the castle.

"You seem unusually quiet, sire," Renbock commented as they walked toward the gate.

"Is it possible, Renbock, that the adventure I've been seeking is not of the body, but of the heart?" the Prince answered as all his thoughts of beasts and dwarves were chased away by the beautiful girl who had just rescued them.

chapter seven

After visiting the mirror, the Queen had decided she needed some new shoes to cheer herself up. The Mirror Queen had put her in a very bad mood indeed, threatening her with vague future consequences. She was pretty sure that the Mirror Queen was bluffing. After all, the Queen had used magic dozens of times and hadn't paid a price yet. But no matter how much she begged, the Mirror Queen still wouldn't give her any gold.

New shoes usually made her feel better, but that day, the servants had shown her almost one hundred pairs and none of them had done the trick. A knock on the door startled the Queen out of her thoughts.

"Your Majesty? You have a visitor," Brighton announced as he walked into the room.

"I'm not in the mood, Brighton," she replied.

"He's young, handsome, and not wearing much clothing," Brighton coaxed.

The Queen lit up. A handsome stranger was just what she needed. "Say no more."

The Queen went down to the great room and settled herself in her throne as Brighton brought in Renbock and the Prince. They both stood quite formally before the Queen, despite their lack of clothing.

"Your Highness, may I present the esteemed Prince of Valencia," Renbock announced.

"Your Majesty," the Prince knelt before the Queen, took her hand, and kissed it regally. "Please excuse our attire. I'm afraid my valet and I were robbed by bandits while traveling through your kingdom."

"Bandits? How awful. How absolutely terrifying . . . and smooth and handsome," the Queen replied, unable to take her eyes off of the Prince. She sighed dreamily as she looked the Prince up and down.

"Er . . . could I bother you for a shawl?" the Prince asked awkwardly, blushing under the Queen's lustful gaze. "Any sort of covering?"

"If you really, really want one," the Queen replied as the Prince nodded. She rolled her eyes. "Fine. Brighton? The Prince is bashful. He requires a shirt."

"Of course, my lady," Brighton replied. Then he turned to face the Prince. "Sir, is there a particular style of shirt you'd—"

"Anything tight and prince-y will do, Brighton," the Queen interrupted. "Thank you."

Brighton bowed and hurried away. The Queen turned her attention completely to the Prince.

"Valencia, you say? I've never heard of it. Is it a wee little hamlet?" she asked.

"Oh no, it's quite a bountiful province, if I say so myself! Quite rich in ore and minerals! Especially gold and silver," the Prince explained.

The Queen smiled—handsome *and* rich—it was her lucky day! But she quickly hid her excitement. Her mind raced with plans to trick the Prince into marrying her. She just needed more information. "You don't say. Please, warm yourself by the fire. You must be freezing." She led the two men over to the fire and they settled into comfortable chairs to talk. "So you're from Valencia. So far from home. Your Princess must be worried sick."

"No, I have yet to wed, Your Highness. . . . I just haven't found the right woman," the Prince answered. Then, thinking of Snow White, he added, "Yet. Your Highness, if I could be so bold as to make a request?"

"'Be so bold' away," the Queen answered flirtatiously.

"These spineless bandits must be brought to justice! And it so happens I've been seeking my princely adventure. If the Queen would permit, I would like to return with an army of my soldiers and personally arrest those thugs."

"Why, that's a wonderful idea. This kingdom could use a little gallantry. Ahh, here is Brighton with some clothes for you," she said.

Brighton handed the Prince and Renbock each a pink spandex shirt adorned with ruffles, shiny white pants, and silver-spangled boots. The two men looked at each other in shock—the clothing was not what they had been expecting, but at least it was clothing. They got dressed quickly with the Queen watching them the entire time.

"Excellent. Then, I'm off!" The Prince stood, finally dressed.

"Don't you look handsome in pink!" The Queen exclaimed sweetly, touching the half-moon pendant around her neck. "You're clearly exhausted. It's already getting late and it's so terribly cold." Renbock was nodding along enthusiastically. A nice dinner, a warm bath, and a soft bed for the night sounded much better than going back into those creepy woods in the dark—they were bad enough during the day. But Renbock looked as if he'd been slapped when the Queen continued, "Your valet can return for reinforcements. And in the meantime, we'll prepare a welcoming ball, befitting a royal prince."

After settling the Prince in a comfortable room and giving Renbock some provisions so he could return for the Prince's army, gold, and some more clothes, the Queen got straight to planning the perfect ball to woo the Prince.

"Send out the invites. Alert the caterer," she ordered Brighton. "I want you to organize a ball like this kingdom's never seen. The Prince is rich, young, and handsome. I'm going to marry him. Then my financial problems will all be solved. But first, I need to sweep him off his feet at this ball."

"How are you going to pay for the party, my Queen?" Brighton asked timidly. "You're broke."

She gave him a dirty look. "Then, go collect more taxes."

"Er, Your Highness," Brighton replied, sweat beading on his forehead, "I don't know the last time you were in the town . . . but the people are starving. . . ."

"Don't you have any imagination? C'mon!" the Queen explained, exasperated, "Tell the villagers that skinny is the new fat. Less is more. Bread is meat! Metaphors, Brighton! Commoners love a good metaphor. Just go sell it."

chapter eight

Meanwhile, Snow had finally made it to the village, lost in a daydream about the handsome young man she'd rescued in the woods. She hoped she might get to see him again someday, even though she doubted it would happen. But when she arrived at the town square, all thoughts of the Prince were driven away.

The town was nothing like she remembered it from her childhood. It used to be a cheerful, prosperous place, but the Queen's constant taxes had taken their toll. The buildings were crumbling and the people were far too thin and dressed in rags. Things were much worse than she ever imagined.

A mother and father with two small children stood by a bakery window, the children staring longingly at the few small loaves of bread in the window. Snow couldn't walk by without offering to help.

"Excuse me," she asked. "What happened here? I once visited with my father, and this was a wonderful place."

"That must have been many years ago," the poor man replied.

His little girl looked up at Snow and asked, "Excuse me, do you have anything to eat?"

"I'm sorry," the mother said, pulling the child away. "She shouldn't have bothered you."

"No, please," Snow replied. She pulled out the lunch she had packed and gave it to the family.

"Thank you," the mother said. She pulled the children along before Snow could change her mind.

Shouts from the square pulled Snow's attention away from the family. The Queen's personal sled had just pulled into town. The bloodred sled with its gold details shone against the dirty snow coating the ground. Snow White looked around frantically for a place to hide. She ducked behind a low wall and flattened herself against it. She could just see what was happening through a small crack in the bricks.

The sled door opened and Brighton, her stepmother's favorite lackey, stepped out with a scroll in hand. The Magistrate hurried out to greet him, clearly fearing the worst.

"More taxes?" the Magistrate gasped when Brighton showed

him the scroll. "What's she doing with all our money?"

The gathered townspeople groaned while Brighton looked around nervously. He hated lying to the villagers.

"Protecting you," Brighton answered.

"Protecting us? From what?"

"From what? Must I remind you of what happened to Old Man Cruthers? Or the gypsy lady from last year? All that was left of her was her tambourine. Even our beloved King was not safe. . . ." Brighton explained, doing his best to sound convincing.

"He's talking about . . ." a townswoman began to say, clearly spooked. The crowd went silent, everyone too afraid to finish the woman's sentence.

"The Beast!" Brighton finally shouted, gesturing with his hands and doing his best to frighten the crowd. "Evil lurks in the dark woods! The only reason it hasn't gorged itself, feasting on your bones, is because your tax dollars are hard at work." He paused for effect. "I'll be back tomorrow for the money. In the meantime, lock your doors. The Queen would be devastated if another life was lost to the vicious beast." Then he marched over to the sled, slammed the door, and headed back to the palace.

Snow shivered as she watched the sled disappear down the path. She knew the Queen wasn't using the tax money to protect the people. She was throwing parties, buying clothes, and ordering lavish feasts that she barely even ate. It made Snow White feel sick. She needed to get back to the castle as fast as she could. She had to do something to help her people. She just had to.

chapter nine

The castle kitchen was a swarm of activity when Snow burst in, her cheeks flushed with cold and anger. All of the weary cooks and servants were chopping, polishing, and preparing the castle for the evening's ball. Snow White wove through the crowd until she found Margaret kneading dough.

"Oh, Margaret, it's worse than you said!" Snow exclaimed, shaking snow out of her hair and pulling Margaret away so they could speak privately.

"You saw the town?"

"Yes, it's awful! The people are so poor. The children are hungry. The Queen has destroyed everything my father believed in!" she sobbed, tears running down her cheeks. Margaret pulled

Snow into a hug and let her sob into her apron. After Snow had cried herself out, she looked around enough to notice how busy the kitchen was.

"What's going on? She isn't throwing another feast, is she?"

"Queen Beelzebub is throwing a party tonight. A costume ball for a special guest: the Prince of Valencia."

"A prince is here?"

"Yes, and, between us, he's very impressive. Easy on the eyes . . . and it's said he has an army!"

Snow's eyes lit up. A powerful prince may have an interest in helping their declining kingdom. She whispered, "Maybe he could help us. If he truly has an army, maybe he could help us take back the kingdom."

"My goodness!" Margaret smiled to see Snow looking so confident and excited. "Someone had quite a day."

"You should have seen the families, Margaret. Those children . . . they need our help." For a moment, Snow looked purposeful and strong. But almost instantly, Snow lost her nerve. "Who am I kidding? No prince would ever give me the time of day."

"Yes, because you're so hard to look at," Margaret teased Snow. "You know, you really are beautiful—much prettier than the Queen. In my experience, handsome princes are about as sharp as butter knives. You just have to use your girlish charm."

Snow sighed heavily. "I don't think I have that."

"If *I* have girlish charms, *you* definitely do," Margaret replied with authority. Snow White blushed and then laughed.

"I actually met someone today, Margaret," Snow admitted with a small smile. "Just briefly. A man."

"Go on."

"He was hanging upside down in his underwear."

"I'm listening."

"It's possible he was the man of my dreams," Snow admitted. Margaret's jaw dropped. "You've really had a big day!"

"I kind of did, didn't I?"

"And you are going to have a bigger night," Margaret continued. "You are going to crash that ball!"

chapter ten

The Queen was leaving nothing to chance for the ball that evening. She knew she needed to look her absolute best if she wanted to catch the Prince's eye. She sat down at her vanity and studied her face closely. She didn't look nearly as young and fresh as she had been when she'd married the King. She pulled at the skin around her eyes and forehead. There were some faint wrinkles and she looked tired. There was no avoiding it—she needed a treatment before the party. Margaret, the baker, was preparing it already.

Just then Brighton came in.

"You look fabulous!" he said.

"'Fabulous'? Brighton, I haven't even begun getting ready

yet," the Queen snapped. "And do I look like I'm dressed for a ball?"

"Well, one can only imagine how fabulous you'll look when —" Brighton backpedaled as quickly as he could.

"Shut up, Brighton."

"With pleasure."

They were interrupted when Margaret came in wearing long rubber gloves and a giant apron. "Your treatment is ready," she announced.

"The treatment? Isn't that a tad excessive?" Brighton asked nervously.

"If my beauty is to remain excessive, then so must my regimen," the Queen sighed as she settled into a reclining chair. "Being the fairest in the land is harder than it looks. Try not to enjoy this, Baker Lady."

"I'll do my best," Margaret answered and then clapped loudly.

The doors to the room opened and a small army of servants holding bags, boxes, and platters came rushing in.

One servant, wearing a mesh mask, carried a golden honeycomb crawling with buzzing bees. Margaret placed the honeycomb on the Queen's lips, causing the bees to sting them over and over again. Soon the Queen's lips were swollen and bright ruby red.

"I can feel you smiling, Baker Lady," the Queen hissed, but it was hard to understand her with such swollen lips.

Margaret turned to hide her smile as she coated the Queen in green mud from a special hot spring deep under the castle and wrapped her in broad leaves from the darkest part of the forest. The mud made the Queen's skin soft and smoothed away any hint of wrinkles, but it smelled like rotten eggs and burned under the leaves.

Next, Margaret pulled two snakes from a black velvet bag. They hissed and writhed as she held their mouths over the Queen's mud-covered face. Both snakes bit into her forehead, the venom from their fangs causing the wrinkles on the Queen's forehead to fill in.

The Queen was plucked, pinched, prodded, stretched, and squeezed until the sun set below the trees and the guests began to arrive for the ball. Then she showered, styled her hair under her most formal crown, slipped into a full-skirted ball gown, and prepared to make her entrance.

🍎 🍎 🍎

Meanwhile, Renbock was racing through the woods back toward Valencia. He felt incredibly conspicuous in his pink and white outfit and urged his horse faster.

"I can't believe the Queen suggested I return to Valencia

alone. At night. Dressed like a circus performer," he grumbled angrily. He looked from side to side nervously, jumping at every snap of a twig or strange noise. "What if the Prince needs me? It's not good for him to be all alone in a strange land—especially not with a queen crazy enough to think this outfit looks good!"

Then suddenly a dark shape began to run along beside him.

Renbock screamed and tried to veer away, but the trees were too thick. The shape caught up to him and then he could see it clearly—a huge dragon beast lunging out of the brush right at him.

"Arghhhhhhhhh!" Renbock's scream tore through the woods.

Then everything faded into silence as a torn pink ruffle floated down to the snowy forest floor.

chapter eleven

The ball for the Prince was the most elaborate party any of the lords and ladies had ever attended. The Queen had instructed each of them to come dressed as an animal, so it looked as though the ballroom had been over-run by a zoo's worth of exotic creatures performing the waltz. A lord in a panda bear tux spun a lady wearing an elephant headdress around the dance floor while two nobles in a horse costume fetched punch for a gaggle of ladies dressed as toucans and a whole herd of women in zebra outfits took appetizers from waiters with lion manes.

When everyone had arrived, trumpets sounded and the Queen made her grand entrance. She looked beautiful in an elaborate gown of lace and ribbons. Everyone cheered and complimented her as she walked down the stairs and over to the waiting Prince, who looked a little silly in a tuxedo with a top hat featuring rabbit ears.

"You were born to wear that hat," the Queen said in greeting, pleased with the costume she had sent up to him.

"I must confess, I feel a bit silly," the Prince said.

"I thought you might find it inspiring for your princely adventures. In folklore, the rabbit is often a character who uses cunning and trickery to outwit his enemies."

"Or perhaps you simply prefer that visiting guests feel slightly ridiculous and uncomfortable so you can have the upper hand?"

"Handsome and smart? How confusing," the Queen laughed, enjoying the flirtatious banter.

As the party went on, the Queen did her best to spend as much time as possible with the Prince, but he kept getting pulled away and she kept getting cornered by the Baron—which worked out perfectly for Snow White.

She had snuck down to the ball and was hiding behind a tapestry with Margaret, trying to work up the courage to talk to the Prince.

"This was a huge mistake. It's a costume party and I've

no costume!" Snow moaned, watching the elegant guests swirl around the dance floor.

"You'll be fine. Let old Margaret sort you out," Margaret said. She looked around for a moment and then grabbed a set of swan wings from a nearby table. Once she had secured them to Snow White's dress, Snow was ready.

Snow took a deep breath and walked into the ballroom. Every head turned as she walked by. In her shimmering evening gown and white swan wings and with the color of her milky white skin, Snow White was the most beautiful woman at the party.

"Snow? Is that you . . . ? You are a sight to behold," a waiter from the kitchen whispered as Snow passed by.

"Oh, thank you," she answered, blushing. "Do you know which one is the Prince of Valencia?"

"I believe he's dancing with Madame Armfelt," the waiter explained, pointing to a woman dressed as a giraffe dancing with a young man wearing a top hat with rabbit ears.

"Oh my! That's the Prince?"

The waiter nodded. Snow felt her heart start pounding wildly. Then she smiled and walked slowly across the dance floor. She turned her head and raised her hand to cover her face as she walked by the Queen, who was dancing with the Baron. The Queen was so focused on escaping from the

Baron that she didn't even notice Snow pass by.

"I heard you taxed the people again," the Baron commented to the Queen.

"Just a wee surcharge," she answered, craning her neck to look for the Prince.

"You know, with my treasury at your disposal, you'd never need to tax the people again. Have you thought any more about my offer of marriage?"

"Oh, Baron, it's positively haunted me."

Just then, the Queen and Baron spun closer to the Prince as the music changed and all of the dancers swapped partners. The Queen turned to partner with the Prince, but a young lady in a shimmering gown cut in front of her and grabbed the Prince's hand. They spun away quickly, leaving the Queen alone in the center of the dance floor without a partner.

As the Prince and Snow White stopped spinning, he got a good look at his partner for the first time and they recognized each other immediately and broke into delighted grins.

"You? You're here!" he exclaimed elatedly.

"I am. I am here," she answered nervously, blushing under his gaze. They both smiled at each other for a moment, saying nothing.

"I apologize. Seeing you in that dress causes me to lose my words."

"At least it doesn't cause you to lose your pants," Snow joked and then scrambled to explain her joke. "I meant because when I met you, you weren't wearing pants."

"I remember. It wasn't my finest hour." He laughed.

"Well, at least now you're dressed. Up"—she smiled—"like . . . a bunny?"

"I prefer rabbit. You see, in folklore the rabbit is often a character who uses cunning and trickery to outwit his enemies."

"Oh. Okay," she agreed seriously, but her eyes were smiling playfully.

"I look like an idiot."

"A little bit, yes."

They both laughed.

"I don't understand, what are you—"

"Doing in the palace? Um, I live here. I have for a while. My whole life actually," she explained. "I'm kind of the Princess."

"B-but, you never told me. . . ." the Prince sputtered.

"As you never told me you were a prince," she countered.

"I feared looking ridiculous," the Prince admitted. Then, after a slight pause, he continued with a laugh. "Said the prince in the bunny rabbit hat."

She laughed as he spun her around and then dipped her in time to the music. Snow was caught off guard. She stumbled, stepping on his foot.

"Ow!"

"Sorry!" she exclaimed, embarrassed. "I haven't danced in a long time."

"Well, I intend to give you plenty of practice this evening," he said flirtatiously, before pausing. "Oh dear, I'm being forward. Surely you have an escort."

"I do now," she smiled.

The Prince deftly twirled her into an embrace, and they locked eyes. They could both feel the sparks between them.

The music changed again and everyone switched partners. The Queen tried to reach the Prince again but the Baron grabbed her hand. The Queen frowned as the Prince spun across the floor with his partner.

"We were supposed to change partners!" Snow exclaimed.

"Were we?" he answered innocently. "How absentminded of me."

Snow looked up and saw the Queen looking in their direction. Uh-oh! She needed to stay out of the Queen's view.

"Dip me again, please. Now," Snow requested.

The Prince obliged, dipping her flawlessly just as the Queen passed by. The Queen couldn't see Snow's face and soon the Baron had spun her to the other side of the room. The Queen did her best to get a good look at the young woman dancing with the Prince, but she couldn't really see his mystery partner.

"Who's that dancing with the Prince?" she demanded, her jealously getting the better of her.

"I wouldn't know. But she's a beauty!" the Baron answered, his eyes wide as he caught a glimpse of her.

Across the room, Snow and the Prince continued to talk as they danced.

"The truth is, I didn't just come here tonight to dance. I came because I need your help," Snow admitted.

"What troubles you? I'm at your disposal," the Prince answered eagerly.

"Well . . . it's the Queen. Since my father died, she's brutalized the people and ruined the land. And I would hope that a Prince as good-hearted as yourself would be able to help me save them."

But just then, the Queen caught a look at Snow White's face. Shaking the Baron's hands off of her, she rushed across the floor toward the couple, weaving around dancing partners. There was no way she was going to allow the interfering little brat to spoil her perfectly laid plans.

"And what exactly do you think you are doing?" the Queen hissed, grabbing Snow White's wrist and pulling her away from the Prince. The music changed just then and the Prince was whisked away by a new partner, who was dressed as a giraffe.

The Queen stared at Snow with her eyes narrowed in a look

of pure hatred. Snow and the Queen moved to the edge of the dance floor. Brighton hurried over to the Queen's side just in time to hear the Queen laugh, a low, evil chuckle.

"Brighton," the Queen said through gritted teeth. "Get. Her. Out. Of."

"Here," he finished. "Yes, I'm on it."

The Prince had flung his dance partner aside and had almost made his way to Snow and the Queen, when the Queen finally let go of Snow's wrist.

"I have to go," Snow whispered to the Prince and then turned and ran, pushing past the guests, out the door.

"Wait!" the Prince yelled.

But Snow was already gone.

chapter twelve

The Queen was furious. She had retreated to a small parlor, where she paced back and forth, her hair escaping from its perfect style and her eyes flashing. Even imagining all the ways she could crush Snow White wasn't helping soothe her.

She paused midstride when a knock sounded at her door. The door opened to reveal two guards carrying Snow White.

"We caught her," the first guard announced.

"You sneaky little girl. Why were you talking to my Prince?" the Queen demanded, her voice low and dangerous.

"Your Prince?" Snow asked.

"And where did you get such a dress?"

Snow was silent for a moment, gathering her courage. "Do

you want to talk about my dress, or about what you did to the village?"

The Queen stepped back as if she'd been slapped. Then she laughed, the same low, evil laugh from the ballroom. "Whoa! Good for you, Snow White!" she said sarcastically. "Someone's been taking her confidence pills. Do that again. Say it again!" She clapped her hands eagerly and then launched into a high-pitched imitation of Snow, "'Do you want to talk about my dress, or about what you did to the village?'"

Snow White just watched her.

"Oh, you're no fun," the Queen continued. "Brighton, you do it, give me your best Snow White!"

"'Do you want to talk about my dress, or about what you did to the village?'" Brighton said immediately in a high-pitched, simpering voice.

"Not irritating enough! Make your voice more irritating, more infuriating, and try again," the Queen demanded.

"'Do you want—'" Brighton began in an even more high-pitched voice.

"Oh, never mind," the Queen interrupted. "The real thing is plenty irritating."

"I've been there. I've seen how you treat the people," Snow continued, refusing to give up. The Queen was stunned.

"You left the castle grounds? Why, Snow White, you little

rebel! You're just breaking all the rules today aren't you? That's a punishable offense."

"By whose law? You have no right to rule the way you do! Technically, I am the rightful leader of this kingdom!" Snow countered with more courage than she ever thought she had.

The Queen's eyes filled with hate. She continued, her voice low and thick with rage, "Hmm. Probably not the best thing you could have said right there. Lock her in her room while I decide how to punish her."

"You can punish me, but we both know the truth," Snow answered bitterly as the guards dragged her away, leaving the Queen and Brighton alone.

"I want her killed," the Queen demanded.

"Y-your Majesty! Isn't that a bit rash?" Brighton sputtered.

"She's a threat to everything. Take her to the woods and feed her to the Beast," the Queen answered, completely unyielding.

Brighton groped for an answer, terrified, and hoping he could somehow change her mind. "Is this about the dress?" he asked.

"I said kill her. And, Brighton?" the Queen answered, stroking the pendant around her neck. "Bring me back proof."

chapter thirteen

Brighton pushed Snow White through the woods, the tip of his knife against her back. She stumbled over a tree root, bare branches scratching her face and pulling at her hair.

"Please don't do this! I'm begging you," Snow whispered, her voice almost lost in the wind. "Just let me go. I'll run away and I swear you'll never hear from me again!"

Brighton was shaking, doing his best to stay in control as he jabbed at her with his knife, forcing Snow to keep moving.

"You think *I* want to be here? You shouldn't have upstaged her, Snow. You know how she is," he said.

An earsplitting howl from the Beast cut through the woods. They both froze. Brighton finally looked around nervously before pushing Snow up against a tree. Holding the knife at her throat and fumbling with a rope, he began to tie her to the tree.

"Please," Snow begged. "I don't want to die as my father did."

The Beast roared again and Brighton looked into Snow's tear-filled eyes. He sighed, dropping the rope.

"Your father was always kind to me," he whispered, all of the fight gone out of him. "Run as fast as you can, Snow. Run as far away from her as you can. Just run."

Then Brighton turned and ran back toward the castle, leaving Snow all alone.

She watched him leave, sobbing, until another roar startled her. Then she turned and ran as fast as she could. She lost the trail and soon found herself tripping and stumbling through thick underbrush. She heard another roar right behind her. When she turned to look, she hit her head on a low-hanging branch and tumbled to the ground. Snow's last thought before she sank into blackness was that she was going to die just like her father.

chapter
fourteen

Brighton rushed back into the castle, sweat dripping from his head and his heart hammering. He couldn't believe what he'd just done. The Queen was going to kill him. He couldn't let her know that Snow was still alive. He needed to cover his tracks—he needed some proof.

Brighton hurried into the empty kitchen. It was almost midnight and the kitchen was deserted. He opened every cupboard and drawer, looking for something. Bread—no. Fruit—no. Cake—no. Finally, he spotted the wooden icebox and wrenched the door open. It was full of raw meat—sausage, steak, ribs.

It was perfect. Brighton grabbed a handful of raw meat chunks and put them into a small sack.

Then he cleaned his hands, wiped the sweat from his brow, and walked into the Queen's chambers.

"Is it done?" the Queen asked, looking up from her vanity. She had been applying moisturizer and putting curlers in her hair. She looked hideous.

"Just as you instructed," he answered, throwing the sack at her feet. The Queen reached down and opened the sack, seeing the meat inside. She looked up, her mouth hanging open.

"That's her liver, her kidney, and a few other assorted parts," Brighton explained.

"Well . . . that's disgusting," she replied, wrinkling her nose at the sight of the blood in the bag. "But, good job, I suppose. I'll admit I'm impressed. You're not as pathetic and wimpy as I believed."

Brighton smiled nervously. *Thank goodness she bought it*, he thought, allowing himself to breath normally again.

The Queen stared at the bag for a moment and then laughed. "Wow. I feel amazing—so relieved. She was so annoying. Always moping around and making everyone sad with her tragic little life story. Brighton, we should have done this years ago. A tricycle accident. Food poisoning. Something. I can't believe it never occurred to me."

"I'm just glad to see you in such a good mood."

The Queen stood and began pacing, thinking of what her

next move should be. "We'll need to release news of the 'tragedy.' You know, the usual, 'What a terrible loss, struck in her youth, blah, blah, blah, a nation mourns. . . .' Maybe fly the flags at half-mast."

Brighton whipped out a pad and paper and took notes. "Flags throughout the kingdom, or just within the palace grounds?"

"Egh, forget the flags. Too much trouble," the Queen mused. "She was really chatting up that Prince. I wonder what she told him? Hmm. Organize a private lunch for me and the Prince. We need to get things back in order. And the sooner, the better."

Snow White was raised by her wicked stepmother, the Queen.

The Queen locked Snow away so she can never steal the title of "Fairest of Them All."

Snow disobeys
the Queen's
orders and
attends a
costume ball.

At the ball Snow is whisked off her feet by a handsome Prince.
It is love at first sight.

The Queen is furious.
She wants the Prince
for herself!

The Queen banishes Snow from the castle.

Snow is scared and runs into the dark woods.
She stumbles and falls.

When she wakes up, Snow finds she has been rescued
by seven dwarves—Grimm, Butcher, Half-Pint,
Chuck, Wolf, Napoleon, and Grub.

Meanwhile, the Queen has slipped the Prince a love potion!

What can break the spell? True love's kiss!

Snow marries her Prince in a fairy-tale wedding.

At the wedding,
a strange old
woman gives
Snow an apple.

The apple is shiny
and red, but Snow
is suspicious.

The old woman is the evil Queen in disguise! Snow feeds her a piece
of the surely poisoned apple and rids her Kingdom of evil forever!

Snow and the Prince live happily ever after.

chapter
fifteen

Snow woke up feeling safe and warm. She didn't want to wake up yet—she was too comfortable. She could hear the crackle of a fire and hear voices murmuring nearby. She thought she could drift back to sleep. Then she remembered what had happened and her eyes fluttered open.

She was in a darkened room with seven men standing over her. She shrieked in alarm.

"She's awake!" one of the men exclaimed. They all stepped back, letting Snow White sit up slowly.

"Who are you?" Snow asked, realizing that they were all dwarves.

"Grimm," said the closest dwarf, his chin resting in his hand. He was clearly the leader.

"I'm Butcher," said a mistrustful-looking dwarf with his sword pointed at her.

"Grub," replied a chubby dwarf between bits of a cream puff.

One dwarf with a carved cane bowed formally before saying, "Napoleon."

"Half-Pint," answered a dwarf who was looking at her with a love-struck expression. He spit into his palm, removed his hat, and smoothed down his hair the best he could, smiling nervously at Snow White.

"Wolf," growled a dwarf with a wolf head on his hat.

"And I'm Chuck," said the last dwarf with a little giggle.

"Now that that's settled, who are you?" Grimm asked gruffly.

"My name is Snow White," Snow answered. Not that who she was meant anything anymore.

"Snow White?" the dwarves all exclaimed at once.

"That's not possible," Grimm said.

"Yeah, Snow White's a defective troll!" Butcher agreed.

Chuck laughed uncontrollably.

Wolf snorted, "They keep her locked up in a tower."

"Maybe this is a different Snow White?" Grub suggested. Everyone else looked at him like he was an idiot. "What? It's not such an uncommon name."

"Name three other Snow Whites you know," countered Butcher.

Grub shrugged.

"If you're Snow White, who's your father?" Napoleon asked.

"The King," Snow answered.

"She *is* Snow White!" Grub exclaimed. He believed her wholeheartedly.

"Grub, don't be an idiot. Anyone pretending to be Snow White would say that," Grimm explained, giving Half-Pint a look.

"Whatever. I say never trust anyone over four feet tall," Butcher grumbled.

"I can't believe we even brought her in at all. One pretty, unconscious girl and we all turn into idiots. Let's drag her back out to the woods and pretend like we didn't see nothin'," Grub suggested.

"No, you fools! If she is a princess, that means she's valuable," Grimm said, a plan already forming in his head.

"We should hold her for ransom. Lots of it!" Wolf exclaimed.

Half-Pint edged closer to Snow White. It was obvious he thought Snow White was very pretty. "Maybe we should get to know her first?"

"You won't get any gold for me!" Snow laughed. "They want me dead! The Queen sent me out here to be killed by the Beast."

"Why'd the Queen want you dead?" Butcher asked skeptically.

"Because she's wicked," Snow answered.

The dwarves all nodded. They had seen the Queen's wickedness firsthand.

"She's evil!" Chuck exclaimed.

"A witch!" Grub agreed.

"Tyrant!" Napoleon nodded.

"Hate her!" Wolf grumbled.

"Sorry, but we've got an appointment," Butcher interrupted, pointing at the clock. "Time for girly to shuffle along."

"Wait! You can't just kick me out," Snow exclaimed. "I have nowhere else to go."

"If the Queen finds you here, she'll kill us, too," Grimm pointed out.

"All I'm asking is to spend one night. Please. First thing in the morning, I'll leave and you'll never see me again," Snow White begged.

They dwarves all looked at one another.

"Huddle!" Grimm shouted. With that, all seven dwarfs rushed together and took a vote. Then the huddle broke apart and they turned to Snow White.

Butcher looked at her, gloating. "Tough luck, Highness."

"Sorry, Snow. All votes need to be unanimous," Grimm explained, as they all turned to give Butcher a dirty look.

"You can glare all you want. I don't care, I'm not changin' my mind," Butcher said, folding his arms over his chest. "I mean it, I'm not stickin' my neck out for some fairy princess."

They all kept staring Butcher down. He nervously pulled at his shirt. He didn't like being the center of attention. Finally, he relented, "Fine. One night."

"Thank you!" Snow exclaimed, clasping her hands together.

"Now, you get some rest and we'll be back later," Grimm said and all seven dwarves marched out the door, stilts in hand.

Once they had left and the door was closed, Snow flopped back down on the bed. What was she going to do?

chapter sixteen

Brighton squirmed uncomfortably as he stood in front of the castle staff. Everyone looked up at him and the room was hushed with anticipation.

"Snow White is dead," he finally announced with a somber expression. He waited a moment while the staff gasped and cried. "One of God's mysteries is his plan for each and every one of us. . . ." he began, but then, seeing the Queen motion for him to hurry up, he finished quickly. "Snow White lived, Snow White died. God rest her soul. Amen!"

Margaret stood to the side with tears streaming down her face.

Later that day, Brighton made the same announcement in the village and posted signs up in the town, looking around every once in a while, half expecting to see Snow White hiding somewhere.

"The Princess is dead? How awful! She was all we had left of our King," a townsman passing by him said.

"Yes, it's terrible. Very upsetting," Brighton answered briskly on his way into the Magistrate's office. "We're all completely broken up."

He knocked on the door and then walked in, surprising the Magistrate.

"Good morning," the Magistrate greeted him.

"I've come for the taxes," Brighton announced.

"The people cannot bear this much longer," the Magistrate said before handing over the bag of tax money.

"You're going to argue about money on this day of grieving? Sir! Have you no shame?" Brighton demanded in mock outrage.

The Magistrate's face fell as he tried to stammer out an explanation. The people really did feel horrible that the poor princess had died. She'd been such a charming child. But Brighton didn't wait to hear it. Instead he took the money and climbed into his waiting sled.

Brighton settled back into the cushions and counted the tax money as the sled sped back to the palace. He hated going to the village and dealing with the poor people there. It always made him feel guilty and vaguely slimy—like he was doing something wrong. But he wasn't. He was just doing his job—at least that's what he always told himself.

At least the tax money he had collected would cover the expenses from the ball. Suddenly, Brighton heard a scream from the front of the carriage and felt the sled come to a jarring stop before flipping over. Brighton and the tax money were thrown through the air and onto the roof of the sled.

They were under attack! Brighton frantically scrambled to put the money back into the bag and then covered his ears, trying not to hear the sounds of swords clanging and yelling outside. Then, just as suddenly, the noise stopped. Brighton scrambled and tried to find a place to hide but it was useless.

The door to the sled opened and Grimm stuck his head inside.

"Well, what do we have here?" he said, yanking a blanket aside to reveal Brighton's hiding spot.

"Looks like a Royal to me," Butcher mused. "Are you a Royal?"

"N-no, no! Not a Royal," Brighton stammered.

"You're riding in the Queen's sled," Napoleon pointed out.

"Oh, is this the Queen's sled? I hadn't noticed. . . ." Brighton answered, looking around as if in surprise.

"And you're wearing royal garments," Grimm added.

"This old rag?" Brighton deflected, "It's a hand-me-down."

"What's in the pretty sack?" Butcher asked.

"My lunch?" Brighton lied, clutching the sack tight.

"Good, I'm famished!" Grub exclaimed. "What are we eating?" Grub snatched the bag, excited for lunch, but he pulled out handfuls of gold instead of food. "Boys! We've found the jackpot!" he exclaimed, tossing the gold coins into the air.

"I'm rich!" Chuck laughed.

"What do you mean 'I'm rich'?" Wolf corrected. "We're rich!"

"Nothing like an honest day's work," Butcher agreed.

"That money belongs to the Queen!" Brighton shouted.

All seven dwarves fixed him with calculating looks. Brighton gulped. He should have kept his mouth shut. "Never mind," he continued. "Don't spend it all in one place!"

chapter seventeen

I t was the dwarves' biggest heist ever and they couldn't wait to spend their stolen gold. The guard uniforms they'd stolen looked pretty dashing on them, too, if they did say so themselves.

As they arrived home, they put their stilts away, as usual. But as soon as they walked into the front door, they realized that nothing was usual inside. Every surface shined and the floors were clean and polished, the table was set for dinner with eight plates, and a delicious smell wafted through the air.

"Welcome back!" Snow White exclaimed. She picked up the stew pot from the stove and ladled its contents into bowls.

"Mmmmm!" Grub sniffed. "Lamb . . . carrots . . . gravy . . . I'd say she's a keeper!"

"Dinner is served," Snow answered, pleased to be of use. Wait, why are you wearing palace guard uniforms?"

"We, uh, got them at work," Napoleon lied.

w looked at each of them in turn before asking, "You
          at the palace. I know everyone who works at the
              d of job do you have?"

                    exchanged nervous glances, but Butcher
                      enegades!"

                    Queen's gold," Grub added sheep-
ishl   old.

"Y   ace?" Snow asked.

"Errr   exactly . . ." Half-Pint answered. "We nabbed it outside the village."

"So you actually stole the people's gold?" Snow glared at him.

"We worked hard for that money!" Butcher countered.

"Stealing isn't work!" Snow scolded. "That's the people's money. They need it! You must return it."

"Sure it's work," Half-Pint replied.

"We had to drag out the stilts," Grimm agreed.

"The sled flipped over," Half-Pint said.

"There was all kinds of fighting!" Napoleon countered.

"I tore my shirt. . . ." Grub added.

"Well, I'm sorry you got a few scrapes, but the townspeople need that money!" Snow insisted.

"Forget them," Butcher scowled.

"They hate us," Grub agreed.

"That can't be true," Snow coaxed.

Wolf shook his head. "It is. They despise us."

"Years ago, when the Queen expelled all the 'undesirables,' no one stood up for us," Grimm explained. "She said, 'Banish all the uglies!' and they did."

Snow shook her head sadly. "I understand you've been mistreated by the Queen. No one understands that more than I do. She locked me up in a tower and never let me leave. It is not fair, the way you've been treated. But neither is stealing from innocent families. My father always said: You can still make the choice to treat others fairly even if others have not done the same for you."

The dwarves listened closely. They knew that Snow had had it hard, but they weren't ready to let go of their old grudge.

"They made us this way, you know," Grimm said, pressing his point.

Half-Pint nodded. "We were legitimate! With real jobs."

"I was a teacher," Grimm said proudly.

"I was a butcher," Butcher admitted.

Wolf stepped forward, too. "We weren't always thieves."

"I ran the pub. A good honest job!" Half-Pint said.

The dwarves were so busy thinking about their past that

74

they didn't notice when Snow White picked up the bag of gold and snuck out the door. Finally though, Grimm looked around and realized they were only talking to each other. He whistled loudly and got everyone's attention.

"After her!" he yelled.

"Get the stilts!" Grub added.

"No time!" Grimm answered.

Then they all took off, chasing Snow through the woods back toward town.

Snow had a good head start on the dwarves and much longer legs, so she made it to the village with time to spare before the dwarves caught up to her. She rushed straight to the Magistrate's office and dumped the gold right onto his desk. He was so surprised to see the gold that it took him a few moments to recognize Snow White. She told him her whole sad story. He was shocked.

"How can I ever repay you, Princess?" he asked.

"Just don't give me away," she begged. "Don't let the Queen know I'm still alive."

The Magistrate wanted to rally the people to help her, but Snow White refused to let them put themselves in danger for her sake, so he agreed to keep her secret. Instead, he went out into the town square to announce the return of the tax money to the people.

"I have a wonderful announcement!" the Magistrate called. "Our money has been returned!"

The townspeople cheered loudly.

"And it was brought to us by . . ." the Magistrate continued, looking around for someone to give the credit to.

Just then the dwarves rushed into the square and Snow White pointed right at them.

"Those men there!" Snow exclaimed, stepping up beside the Magistrate. She knew the people wouldn't recognize her. After all, none of them had recognized her on her last trip to the village. "The Queen told you they were undesirable, but the Queen lied!"

The crowd turned to see the dwarves.

"Those brave men are the true heroes," Snow continued. "They fearlessly raided the Queen's caravan and retrieved your gold! They're the ones who deserve your thanks!"

"Oh no, that's not what happened!" Grub corrected Snow. "We stole the money for ourselves!"

"Grub!" Grimm exclaimed, elbowing Grub in the ribs. "Shut up."

Grub shut up immediately, blushed, and then gave the crowd a small wave.

The crowd burst into cheers again and everyone rushed to thank the dwarves.

"It's so good to see you again!"

"The pub hasn't been the same without you!"

"We've missed you!"

The dwarves were so surprised, and also excited to learn that they'd been wrong about the villagers. The crowd grew bigger around them as they were showered with generous praise and gratitude.

One by one, the dwarves looked up at Snow White and smiled.

chapter eighteen

The Queen didn't waste any time wooing the Prince once Snow White was out of the way. She invited him to a special, private lunch in the most regal dining room right after Snow White's death was announced to the staff.

"Are you enjoying your partridge?" the Queen asked sweetly.

"It's very tasty, Your Majesty," he answered.

"We're beyond such formalities," she cooed. "Call me Gertrude. You know, everyone remarked what a wonderful dancer you were last night."

"Thank you, Your Majesty. Er . . . Gertrude," he replied, but his thoughts drifted to his dance with Snow White. "I do have one question about the evening. There was a girl with black hair. She was very beautiful."

"Beautiful?" the Queen asked. This was the conversation she'd been dreading.

"The most beautiful girl I've ever seen."

"*Ever* is a very long time."

"No! I know it with all my heart. She is the most beautiful girl in the world."

"Agree to disagree, let's leave it there," the Queen said coldly.

"Do you know her? Skin like ivory, black hair," he continued, oblivious to the Queen's growing anger.

"Her hair is not black. It's raven. And she's eighteen and she's never seen the sun. Of course she's got good skin!" the Queen snapped, almost crushing her glass with her clenched fist. Then she caught herself and took a deep breath. She couldn't afford to let the Prince know how much she loathed her stepdaughter. "The girl you speak of is named Snow White," she finished sweetly.

"Ah! She is very well suited to her name!"

"Yes, an unfortunate case. That child wasn't all . . . there," the Queen lied, feigning sadness.

"She's crazy?"

"Some say crazy, some say 'mentally deficient.' She even thought she was the Princess!" the Queen laughed.

The Prince was dumbfounded. Snow White had seemed so genuine, so charming, so perfect. "Why, yes. She did mention that!"

"She suffered from flights of fancy. She believed I stole the kingdom, ruined the land, and spoiled the crops."

"Why do you refer to her in the past tense?" he asked.

"Oh, have I been? How indelicate of me," the Queen replied. "You obviously haven't heard the sad news."

"What news?"

"She's dead."

"Dead! What? How?"

"It happened last night, in the woods. They are such a treacherous place," the Queen shuddered, pretending to be heartbroken.

"This is terrible!" The Prince had gone ashen.

"Do you need a second?" The Queen asked, sounding genuinely concerned.

"Yes, thank you."

The Queen waited exactly one second, and then continued, "I have a proposition for you, Prince. We're both single adults, roughly the same age. . . ."

"I don't think we're the same age," the Prince interjected, though his mind was still on Snow White.

"I said 'roughly.' Point is — the clock is ticking for both of us. We're both people of means. Leaders with lands," she coaxed. "So my question is this: Would you do me the honor of being my—"

A loud rapping at the door cut the Queen off mid-question. She was furious, but couldn't let the prince see. "Give us a moment, please?" she called out with fake sweetness.

But the door opened anyway and Brighton walked in, blushing and clad only in his underwear. "Your Highness, there's been a development. The royal taxes have been stolen."

"Stolen?" the Queen demanded. "By whom?"

"By . . . uh . . . bandits," Brighton stammered.

The Prince gave Brighton a sharp look. He knew exactly what had happened. "By . . . bandits?" he asked and gestured to a height of four feet tall behind the Queen's back.

Brighton nodded, ashamed. "Uh-huh. Bandits. Very intimidating ones."

The Prince took the opportunity to escape the Queen and jumped to his feet, "I'm sure those were the same bandits that attacked me and my valet. I cannot wait any longer. Enough with those cowardly muggers! Justice must prevail!"

"Wait!" the Queen shouted. She had been so close to her proposal. "What about your dessert?"

"Put my dessert on ice. I will go do the same to those dwarv . . ." he announced, then caught himself. "Those . . . cowardly bandits!"

chapter nineteen

The dwarves were thrilled to have their old friends and neighbors back. Almost all of them wanted to invite Snow White to live with them. After all, she didn't have anywhere else to go and they really liked her, but Butcher still wasn't convinced that Snow White should stay.

"Deal's off. She stole our money!" Butcher yelled that night after dinner. "She can spend the night with the Beast for all I care."

"But now the people like us," Chuck countered.

"She's a good cook," Grub threw in.

"Guys, c'mon! We've been welcomed into town, she's politically connected, and she's got spunk!" Grimm said definitively.

Half-Pint looked at Snow White dreamily, "What's not to like?"

"I demand a revote," Butcher insisted.

"You can't demand a revote," Grub snapped, then turned to Grimm and whispered, "What's a revote?"

"Huddle!" Grimm yelled. All of the dwarves huddled together to vote. After a few minutes they broke apart and called Snow White in. She'd been waiting outside.

"You can stay," Grimm announced.

"Oh, thank you!" She exclaimed.

Butcher pushed his way forward and held up his hand for Snow White to pause. "But we got conditions. If you're gonna live with us, you gotta be one of us."

"I have to be a . . . dwarf?" Snow White asked.

"No, no!" Napoleon answered. "He means you must be a thief."

"A thief?" Snow shook her head. "I could never do that."

"How about . . . a burglar?" Half-Pint suggested.

Snow paced back and forth, "I feel I've been pretty clear about my thoughts on stealing."

The dwarves looked back and forth at one another. There had to be a way around Snow's moral objections. Suddenly, Wolf had an idea. "What if you were stealing from the Queen?"

Snow White looked up—it was a good point.

"You said yourself that she's wicked," Grimm coaxed.

Grub agreed, "Somebody has to stop her."

"Why not you?" Napoleon added.

"Why not us?" Half-Pint said, getting into the spirit.

Snow nodded. It wasn't such a bad idea. Someone needed to help the villagers and stand up to the Queen. Why couldn't it be her? "I had hoped that the Prince would make things right, but maybe together we can find a way to stop her?" She smiled. "But this time, *I* have conditions. Whatever we steal goes back to the people."

All the dwarves nodded.

"Minus a small commission. I'm just talkin' expenses," Butcher protested, but relented under his friends' glares. "Fine. We'll do it out of the goodness of our thieving hearts."

"Group hug!" Half-Pint yelled and they all embraced, Butcher still grumbling in the middle.

"But she doesn't know the first thing about thieving," Butcher gave one last feeble protest.

"Then we'll teach her," Grimm answered.

"Yeah. We'll teach her how to think small!" Wolf exclaimed.

The dwarves worked nonstop to teach Snow everything they knew over the next few days.

Grimm taught her how to duel. "People say you can't be tall if you're short, that you can't be strong if you're not. But a weakness is only a weakness if you think of it that way," he explained as he showed her how to use her supposed weaknesses to gain the advantage over her opponents. "Never, under any circumstances, cede the high ground." Before long, she could beat any of the dwarves with a sword.

Napoleon taught her how to make an impression on her enemy. "If your enemy fears the way you look, the battle's already won," he coached. Snow White ditched her dresses and demure look for a leather battle suit and a tough-girl new hairstyle, designed to strike fear into the Queen's heart. She looked amazing!

Wolf showed Snow how to win in hand-to-hand combat. "People think of you as sweet. They don't expect you to fight dirty. Use that to your advantage," he instructed. Soon Snow could pin him in seven seconds flat.

Chuck was an expert in improvisation and he taught Snow how to use anything around her to help her win a fight, "Your weapon isn't your only friend. The environment can be an ally, too." So Snow became an expert at turning anything into a weapon, and turned into an ace with a slingshot.

Grub showed Snow White how to trick her enemies with sleight of hand. "Deception on the battlefield isn't just an option.

Oftentimes, it's the difference between victory and defeat." Snow White knew she'd need some tricks up her sleeve since the Queen wouldn't hesitate to fight dirty.

Finally, the dwarves had taught her all they could. Snow White and the seven dwarves were ready for battle.

chapter twenty

The Prince was ready for battle, too. He gathered a group of the Queen's guards and led them into the forest to face the fearsome "bandits." He wished he had Valencia's guards at his back, but he was hoping the Queen's guards would fight as fiercely as his own.

"The bandits were somewhere in this region," the Prince announced when they reached the spot where he and Renbock had been attacked. He pushed through the trees, looking for tracks, and was surprised to see a figure wearing a hooded cloak on the path. It looked like it might be an old woman. She had dropped her market basket and seemed to be having trouble gathering up her things. "Ma'am, can I offer you assistance?" he asked, striding over to help her. As a prince, he felt it was his duty to help anyone in need, especially someone alone in the dangerous woods.

But when the old woman looked up, he was face-to-face with a beautiful young girl—it was Snow White! He was elated.

"It's . . . you!" he stammered. "I thought you'd been killed."

"I almost was," she admitted. She was just as surprised to see him as he was to see her.

He reached out and took her hand in his. She smiled up at him. He smiled down at her and then leaned toward her. But, just at that moment, the dwarves on their stilts jumped out of the trees overhead, spoiling the moment.

"Give us your valuables!" Butcher yelled.

The Prince drew his sword and jumped in front of Snow White, ready to protect her. "Stay behind me and you'll be safe! Stay away, you foul bandits. You shall not harm this innocent maiden."

Grimm laughed and tossed Snow her sword, "Here you go, innocent maiden."

The Prince turned, startled, "Wait! You're with the bandits?"

"Wait! You're with the Queen?" Snow asked, shocked.

"You are a traitor!"

"And you're a jerk!"

With that, Snow White attacked. She couldn't believe the Prince was siding with the Queen. The dwarves were holding their own against the Prince's guards, leaving Snow White and the Prince all alone.

"Stop this at once! I can't fight you!" the Prince said, sticking to defensive moves as Snow's swordplay backed him down the path.

"Why not?" she asked.

"You're a girl! I don't fight girls."

She sliced her blade across his chest, tearing his shirt. "Perhaps you should reconsider. I hate to burst your bubble, but I'm not so innocent."

The Prince finally gave in and charged, forcing her to back up.

"The Queen said you were crazy!"

"The Queen's often wrong. She also said I was dead," Snow countered. They continued to argue as they crossed swords, turning and jabbing their way through the trees.

"The Queen has you in her thrall. Can't you see she's manipulating you?"

"That's absurd."

"She needs your wealth to save her from ruin!"

"The Queen would be fine if your friends would stop robbing her," he insisted. "Yield!"

"Never!"

Suddenly, the Prince knocked her off balance and

she stumbled. He thrust his blade against her throat.

"Do you yield?" he demanded.

Snow White dropped her gaze and her sword. She sighed. "Okay, yes. I yield."

The Prince dropped his sword ready to accept her surrender, but as soon as he did, Snow White kicked his legs out from under him and flipped on top of him. They grappled, both trying to grab their swords.

The dwarves had surrounded the guards and were busy tying them up when they noticed Snow struggling with the Prince.

"We have to help her!" Half-Pint yelled.

"I dunno. She's doin' pretty good on her own," Butcher replied, impressed.

Finally, Snow and the Prince rolled to a stop, out of breath.

"If you weren't working with my sworn enemy, I'd probably kiss you right now," the Prince gasped.

"If you weren't working with my sworn enemy, I'd probably let you," Snow countered, smiling flirtatiously before kneeing him hard.

The Prince groaned and let her go. She hopped up and turned to leave. She had won—all those lessons had paid off. She looked back to see how the dwarves were doing, but when she caught a glimpse of the Prince moaning on the ground, she felt horrible. She couldn't just leave him like that. "Forgive me," she said, reaching out to help him up.

"No," he groaned. "Forgive me." Seeing his chance, the Prince picked up a handful of snow and threw it in Snow's face. She dropped to the ground. He had been faking the entire time! The Prince hopped up, grabbed his sword, and pointed it at Snow. "You've been bested."

Snow frowned. Then she whipped around and threw a rock right at him. Unfortunately, she missed.

"Ha! You throw like a girl!" the Prince laughed.

But Snow hadn't been aiming at the Prince and her rock did hit its target—a nearby tree. The rock knocked loose the snow from the tree's branches, which landed on the Prince's horse, startling him so that he kicked the Prince.

The Prince dropped to the ground again, truly dazed. Snow ran over to him. She reached down and pushed his hair off his forehead, hoping he'd be too woozy to stop their raid and that she wouldn't have to hurt him again. But the Prince just wouldn't quit. He tried to stand up.

"Oh, why do you have to be so cute?" she asked, before she walloped him with a punch that knocked him out cold.

chapter twenty-one

The Prince was blushing so fiercely that he was sure he looked like a tomato, and his head was pounding from Snow White's last punch. He hated to admit it, but she had really kicked his butt. It was so embarrassing.

He and the guards were standing in front of the Queen, and once again he was wearing nothing but his underwear. The dwarves had stolen all of their clothes and gold — again. The Queen was furious.

"Really, Prince," she said through clenched teeth. "We have to stop meeting this way."

"The bandits caught us by surprise," he explained sheepishly.

"You went into the woods to find the bandits, yet the bandits still caught you by surprise?" she asked.

The Prince frowned. "Yes, Gertrude."

"Let's go back to 'Your Majesty' for the moment."

"Y-your Majesty," he continued, "I must admit, we were out skilled. Their leader was brutally ruthless. She was—"

The Queen cut him off, "She? The bandits' leader is a girl?"

"Yes. The bandits' leader is . . ." the Prince trailed off, realizing that the Queen did not know Snow White was still alive. He had a feeling that the Queen would not take that news well. He tried to think of a cover, but the Queen was watching him like a hawk. There was no way he could lie— she would see right through him. "The bandits' leader . . . is Snow White."

Brighton stepped forward immediately, trying to cover, "Impossible. Snow White is dead. Perhaps it was someone who just looked like Snow White."

"It was definitely Snow White," the Prince insisted.

"I think we should at least open ourselves up to the possibility that it was just someone who looked a lot like Snow White," Brighton pleaded. The Queen was looking back and forth between them, her eyes flashing with fury. "No? No chance of that?"

The Queen turned on Brighton, her voice as cold as ice, "Well, this is a fun surprise."

The Prince stepped forward. He was furious, too. "You told me she was dead!"

The Queen pointed at Brighton. "He told ME she was dead!"

"I thought she was dead!" Brighton insisted.

"You also said she was mad!" the Prince demanded of the Queen.

"Oh, she's mad," the Queen answered. "Not as mad as I am, however."

"So which is it, mad or dead?" the Prince asked. "To me, she appeared quite sound of mind as she led her bandit band of dwarves."

"Dwarves?" the Queen shrieked. "You said they were giants!"

The Prince had forgotten that little detail in his mission to get answers. He blushed again. "Oh! Er, they were giant . . . dwarves! Sometimes they're big, sometimes they're small."

The Queen was not happy at all. Snow White was not dead. Brighton had lied to her. And the giant bandits turned out to be dwarves. "I have been deceived," she hissed.

"*I* have been deceived," the Prince countered. "I have been misled either by you or by Snow. And I find this odd turn of events quite confusing."

"Yes, 'confusing' is a fine word, a grand word for this situation! Years from now, when people reflect upon the word 'confusing,' they will point to this particular afternoon, when the world learned that a dead girl was alive, leading a group of big small people!" she screamed. Then she stood up and marched out of the room, leaving a stunned silence behind her.

The Queen had never been so furious. She rushed through the castle and into her private rooms. It was time to visit her mirror.

"Is she really alive?" The Queen demanded as soon as she faced the Mirror Queen.

"I was going to tell you," the Mirror Queen answered, perfectly calm. "But I thought it would be more entertaining to let you find out on your own. As usual, I was right."

The Queen scowled at the mirror. "I don't understand! Why is there a growing disconnect between what I believe and what is real? Brighton said he fed her to the Beast," the Queen sputtered.

"Brighton fell victim to her beauty, like all the others. He felt bad for poor, lovely, beautiful Snow White."

The Queen groaned. She was in serious trouble. Snow White was almost as beautiful as she was—if not more beautiful. The Prince was slipping out of her grasp and she couldn't even control her own servants anymore.

"I need your magic," the Queen said quietly.

"There is a price for using my magic."

"What is this 'price' you're always going on about? Do you always have to be so cryptic? I just want her dead."

"Just dead? No matter the cost?" the Mirror Queen asked.

"Oh, and I want Brighton dead, too."

"Don't overreact. Kill Brighton and you'd be without your executive bootlicker."

"He has to be punished for lying! Do something terrible to him. Use your magic!"

"So shortsighted. You will pay the—"

"I'll pay the price for using magic, yes," the Queen interrupted. "I've got it. Now punish him!"

The Mirror Queen shrugged, and then snapped her fingers.

Meanwhile, Brighton was walking to his room, sweating as he worried about how the Queen would punish him. Then suddenly he was enveloped in a cloud of smoke. He felt himself shrinking down, down, down.

When the smoke cleared, nothing seemed the same. Brighton looked down, but his antennae got in the way. He wasn't a person anymore; he was a cockroach. The Queen had turned him into a bug! He let out a cockroach squeal and scurried down the hall, hoping no one would step on him.

The Queen watched Brighton become a cockroach in the mirror and then snapped her fingers gleefully. "So what do I do about this Prince?" she demanded.

The Mirror Queen raised one perfectly arched eyebrow. "Forget the Prince. Perhaps the Baron is more your speed."

"No! I have to marry the Prince!"

"That's impossible. His heart yearns for Snow White," the Mirror Queen replied.

The Queen paced back and forth. She was losing her grip. "Then give me the love potion from before! The one I served to her father!"

"You used it up. You've used up too much."

But the Queen refused to give up. She couldn't stop now. "Just give me whatever you got!"

When a vial appeared in her hand, the Queen shrieked with glee while the Mirror Queen watched, shaking her head in disapproval.

chapter twenty-two

Once the Queen had her love potion, she sent a servant to bring the Prince up to her quarters. Before he arrived though, she pulled out two goblets—one gold and one silver—and filled them both with wine. Then she pulled out the vial of love potion and added it to the silver goblet. She quickly fixed her hair and she was ready.

She had just finished powdering her nose when the Prince knocked on the door and came in. "Your Majesty, you wanted to see me?" he asked.

"Thank you for coming. I feel terrible about our little quarrel before. It's been a trying day and I . . . overreacted," she said sweetly, offering him the silver goblet. "Here, have a peace offering. It's delicious."

"No, thank you. I don't feel like drinking."

"And that's because you are a man in love?" the Queen coaxed gently.

The Prince was surprised. He hadn't realized the Queen was that perceptive. "Is it that obvious?"

"The look in your eyes when you speak of Snow White," the Queen said. "It may surprise you, but despite my crown, I can be a wise counsel in matters of the heart."

The Prince sighed. "Oh! I just don't understand, Your Majesty! When I met her in the forest, she seemed so kind. Then at the dance, she was lovely and charming. But then today . . ."

"Her true colors were revealed?" the Queen finished.

"Yes. I suppose so."

"Snow White's a very erratic girl," the Queen said, doing her best to sound sympathetic. "Some would call her high maintenance."

"Love is so difficult," the Prince complained.

"Love always is. I thought I'd found myself the ideal man, and then he was struck down in his prime," she confided, letting her eyes fill with fake tears. "In fact, it was on this very day, four years ago—no, two years ago—somewhere in that range . . . anyhow, it's when I lost my beloved husband."

"I'm so sorry to hear that."

"I had wished to toast him tonight, but drinking alone can be rather sad," the Queen said.

"You are right!" the Prince answered. He couldn't let the poor Queen suffer alone. "We must honor the late King. A fallen hero must be remembered."

The Prince grabbed for the gold goblet—the one without the love potion. The Queen reached out and grabbed his wrist before he could take a sip. "N-no! Gold is my lucky color."

She handed the Prince the silver goblet instead. He raised his glass in a toast, "To love lost."

"To love gained," the Queen replied flirtatiously.

She smiled broadly as he took a long sip from his goblet. There was a flash of light and the Prince was under her spell. The Queen stood, ready for the Prince's proposal, but instead he dropped to the ground and rolled on his back. Then he scratched an itch on his ear—with his foot. Something was not right.

"What are you doing?" she shrieked.

The Prince, on hearing her voice, jumped up and rushed over to her. He frantically kissed and licked her face and neck.

The Queen pushed him off of her and shouted, "Calm down. Calm down! Ughh—sit!"

The Prince immediately sat and stared up at her with puppy eyes. The love potion was not supposed to work like that. She pulled out the potion vial and examined the label more closely. It had a small picture of a dog on one side with the words "Puppy Love" written over the picture in cursive.

"Puppy Love? Puppy! What am I supposed to do with a puppy?" she muttered to herself.

With her guard down, the prince immediately attacked her, covering her in puppy kisses. She laughed uncontrollably.

"You and I will have such fun!" the Prince said between kisses. "You can take me on walks! You can throw sticks, and I'll retrieve! You can scratch my tummy!"

"All off topic," the Queen said. She had finally regained control and was holding him at arm's length. "What I need is for you to marry me."

"Sure! I'll do that! I'll love you to the four corners of the earth! I'll love you to the edges of the Seven Seas and beyond! Let's get married!" the Prince exclaimed. "You are my master!"

The Prince leapt around the room, wiggling with excitement. It was more than the Queen could take. She looked around frantically until she found a candlestick. She grabbed it and threw it out the window, yelling "Fetch!"

The Prince ran out of the room, eager to fetch for her.

The Queen collapsed into a chair. The puppy love potion wasn't perfect, but it had done the trick. She was getting married. There was only one thing left to do. "And now the final loose thread. We get rid of Little Miss Sunshine," the Queen whispered to herself.

chapter twenty-three

The Mirror Queen was scary when she was performing magic. She sat cross-legged and blindfolded on the floor surrounded by candles arranged in mystical patterns. The flames sputtered and wavered as she set two faceless mannequins with buttons for eyes holding hammers in front of her. She chanted over them waving her arms and moving her hands in a series of complicated motions, "Wicked dolls with button eyes, wake and stretch, tonight you rise, then go and bring the girl's demise."

As she chanted, the mannequins glowed and then sat up. Shimmering strings appeared, stretching from the mannequins to the Mirror Queen and connecting them with her magic. She lifted her hands and the mannequins stood up. Then she smiled a very wicked smile. Snow White wasn't going to know what hit her.

Deep in the forest, Snow White and the seven dwarves were celebrating their successful raid over dinner.

"I gotta admit: Snow turned out to be a great fighter," Grub said between bites of stew.

Grimm laughed. "You mean, we turned out to be great trainers! To us!" he cheered, raising his glass for a toast.

But Butcher didn't raise his glass. He hated that they had given all of the gold to the villagers instead of keeping it for themselves and he was still sulking. "I don't see why you're all celebrating. We risked our lives for nothing."

Just then Half-Pint rushed in, clearly worked up. He'd gone to drop off their spoils at the village. "You won't believe what I just heard at the pub!" he exclaimed without even greeting his friends. "The Queen is getting married!"

"No way!" Chuck shouted. "That's crazy!"

"Who's she marrying? The Baron?" Snow asked.

"The Baron? No!" Half-Pint replied. "She's marrying the Prince!"

Snow White suddenly felt like all of the air had disappeared from the tiny room. "W-why would he do that?" she stammered. "W-when is the wedding?"

"It's tomorrow, on the lake," Half-Pint answered. "A private little affair that she's invited every noble to."

Snow White stood up and ran out of the room. She needed to be alone. After throwing the front door open, she rushed down the path, letting tears fall onto the snowy ground. Finally, she stopped and sat against a large oak tree, not caring that the snow was soaking through her cloak. She buried her face in her hands and let herself cry. She felt so stupid—how could she have thought the Prince loved her? She was a nobody. Of course he'd rather marry the Queen.

Snow was so busy crying that she failed to notice two mannequins as tall as she was glide silently along the path behind her toward the dwarves' cottage.

Inside, the dwarves were trying to figure out what was wrong with Snow White.

"What was that about?" Wolf asked.

"Idiot. Can't you see? She loves him," Napoleon sighed. "Poor Snow."

"Loves him? He tried to kill her today," Grub exclaimed.

"Exactly! What do you think love is?" Napoleon replied matter-of-factly.

"She can't love him," Half-Pint protested. "She should be with someone . . . shorter!"

Napoleon shook his head. He could tell Half-Pint was smitten with Snow. "Somebody has to see if she's okay."

"She's a girl. Girls cry. No big deal," Butcher said, helping himself to another bowl of stew.

While the others were arguing, Grub was busy eating. As he reached for the potatoes, he saw movement through the window. It looked like two large dolls. But that couldn't be right, could it?

Then a blank face with button eyes popped up in front of the window. Grub tried to scream, but his mouth was too full of food. He waved his hands, squeaking and sputtering, finally spitting his mouthful of potatoes at Butcher.

"What now, Grub?" Butcher demanded, wiping potatoes off his face.

Grub pointed at the window and yelled, "Black magic!"

The first mannequin smashed through the window. The dwarves all screamed in surprise, but quickly rallied, grabbed their weapons, and poured out of the house, ready to fight.

Butcher, Half-Pint, and Grub tackled the first mannequin while Grimm, Wolf, Napoleon, and Chuck went for the second. The mannequins fought like they couldn't feel pain, rebounding easily from every blow and kick. The dwarves were outmatched for the first time they could remember. They needed to retreat and regroup.

Butcher, Half-Pint, and Grub dashed back into the safety of the house. They slammed the door shut and barricaded it with furniture.

"Wait! What about Snow White?" Half-Pint yelled.

"She'll be safe in the woods!" Butcher answered. "Come on. We need to get upstairs to the high ground!"

They rushed up the steps, but stopped when they saw the first mannequin drop down through a hole in the ceiling. It had climbed up the side of the house in a matter of moments. Butcher jumped off the steps, kicking the mannequin and knocking it over. It fell to the ground with a thump.

"I think I got it," Butcher exclaimed. "It's out cold!"

Half-Pint hugged him in relief. But then the mannequin stood back up. Its head spun around and it gave a shake. It was ready for action again. The dwarves ran for the bedroom area, hiding under their bunks. The mannequin smashed at each bed while the dwarves rolled back and forth, just barely avoiding the blows.

Meanwhile, Grimm, Wolf, Napoleon, and Chuck ducked into a nook in a tree. It was too small for the mannequin to get into. After trying in vain to pull them out, the mannequin began hacking at the tree with its hammer.

"Is that what it feels like to be a nail?" Napoleon yelled frantically.

Suddenly, the mannequin quit and spun around, its attention on something else. Grimm peeked out of their hiding spot to see Snow White fighting the mannequin. She had her gold knife out and was getting in some good hits. But the mannequin never slowed down. After a few moments, Snow White paused staring above the mannequin at the inky black sky. He couldn't figure out what she was doing.

"Don't look up there, dummy!" Grimm yelled. "Look at the mannequin!"

But Snow looked over at him and winked. He followed her gaze and saw that a set of shimmering strings went from the mannequin up into the air. The dwarves had been so busy trying to save themselves that they hadn't noticed that. Snow flipped though the air and sliced right through the strings with her knife.

Back at the castle, the Mirror Queen recoiled as if someone had cut her.

"Ouch!" she yelled. She inspected her hand. A red cut had appeared on her palm and was bleeding. When Snow White cut those strings, she had cut the Mirror Queen, too.

Snow White, Grimm, Wolf, Napoleon, and Chuck raced into the house. They found the second mannequin hacking at the last remaining bed. Butcher, Half-Pint, and Grub were hiding underneath it, trembling with fear. The mannequin raised its hammer, ready to strike the killing blow, when Snow White reached above it and slashed its strings. The mannequin fell forward onto the bed, no longer a threat.

"Is everyone OK?" Snow asked.

Grimm looked around, counting heads. "Yep. We've got a few minor injuries, but we're all here."

Snow White felt horrible. Her friends were bruised and battered and their home was a wreck—it was all her fault. The Queen had to have sent those mannequins for her. The dwarves could have been killed just because they'd helped her. "If it wasn't for me, none of this would have happened," she sighed.

"If it wasn't for you, we'd be dead right now," Butcher corrected her.

The dwarves all piled around Snow in a group hug. She was lucky to have them, but she couldn't keep putting them in danger. Snow knew what she had to do.

chapter twenty-four

The next morning, the dwarves all woke up sore and tired. Those mannequins had really beat them up. Napoleon was the first one to get up. His stomach growled and he crossed his fingers that Snow White had made them breakfast. He went to the kitchen to look for her, but she was gone.

"Snow must have left while we slept!" Napoleon yelled up to the others.

Half-Pint padded downstairs sleepily, "Impossible. She'd never just leave like that. . . ." He looked around. Snow really was gone.

"Did she make us breakfast?" Grub asked. "I could sure use a tall stack of pancakes."

"No, but she left a note," Half-Pint said. He picked up a note from the table in Snow's neat handwriting and read it out loud. "'Dear Butcher, Napoleon, Grub, Half-Pint, Wolf, Chuck, and Grimm. I'm so sorry to leave. I love you all dearly but I've realized my presence can only cause you harm. I thought I was strong enough to do this, but I am not.'" He paused, tears welling up in his eyes. "'I am not my father, much as I wish I was. I am not a leader. I'll go someplace far away where I can be safe from the Queen, but I know I will forever cherish our time together. Love, Snow. P.S. Grub, I left you a tall stack of pancakes on the stove.'"

By the end of the letter, all of the dwarves are crying. They couldn't believe Snow was really gone.

"I don't want pancakes anymore," Grub wailed. "I just want Snow back!"

"We need to go after her," Napoleon exclaimed.

They all rushed out the door, planning to hunt Snow White down, with Grimm in the lead. But no sooner had he opened the door then he found Snow White repairing the sign outside of their house that read: WARNING: YOU MUST BE SHORTER THAN 48 INCHES TO ENTER. He stopped short, forcing all of the other dwarves to run into his back and fall to the ground in a heap.

"Snow!" Grimm exclaimed as his friends picked themselves back up. They were all so relieved to see Snow.

"I'm sorry, guys, I just can't keep putting you all in danger," Snow insisted. "I need to leave the kingdom altogether so the Queen will leave you alone."

"You can't just give up now! What about the Prince?" Napoleon demanded.

"He loves someone else," she answered sadly.

"That's impossible! How could anybody love the Queen more than they love you?" Grub said.

Snow shook her head, "I was foolish. I never had a chance with the Prince just like I never had a chance against the Queen. She's too powerful, too smart. I'm just a girl. . . ."

"No," Butcher insisted. "If the Queen marries the Prince, we'll all be doomed to suffer—forever. C'mon! You've got to stop the wedding!"

"Yeah," Grimm added. "If not for love, then do it for the people."

Snow was moved by their sincerity, and their faith in her. They were right. How could she give up on herself so easily? She was being selfish. The people needed her. "I never thought I'd be lectured on social responsibility by a bunch of thieves," she teased them.

"You told us once that just because the world isn't fair to us, we still can steal from people as long as they're not poor children," Napoleon said, looking her in the eyes.

Grimm rolled his eyes, "That's not what she said."

"I'm taking poetic license," Napoleon responded, "But seriously, Snow, you took seven thieving dwarves who thought they had no other choice in life, and you gave them another choice. You were strong enough to do that."

Butcher put his arm around her shoulders. "We don't see a little girl when we look at you, Snow. . . ."

"We see a princess," Grimm finished. He pulled out his sword.

Chuck pulled his sword out, too. "And a leader."

"Our leader," Butcher added, holding out his sword.

"Your kingdom needs you," Grub insisted with his sword in hand.

"I need you," Half-Pint continued, looking at her lovingly. "Uh. I mean, we need you."

She looked at each of them for a moment, then proudly pulled out her own sword, "Who feels like crashing a wedding?"

chapter twenty-five

The Queen and Prince's wedding party was an extremely elaborate affair. All of the lords and ladies of the kingdom were in a pure white tent set atop a large frozen lake near the castle. White twinkling lights crisscrossed over the tent's roof and exotic flowers were arranged in crystal vases on every table. The guests enjoyed champagne and hors d'oeuvres while they waited for the wedding to begin.

The Prince greeted each guest as they arrived, telling each of them how excited he was about the marriage. "I can't wait to marry the Queen. Yes, she is the most beautiful woman I've ever met."

Of course, plenty of the Nobility were gossiping about the strange pairing. It was awfully odd that the Queen was marrying the young prince after only a few days.

"He's very attractive," a noblewoman whispered to the Baron.

"Though a bit . . . young for her, don't you think?" he replied.

They watched as the Prince took a lady's hand, and then eagerly licked it.

"That must be how they do it in Valencia," the Baron mused.

With so many guests milling about, it was easy for the dwarves to sneak into the party in disguise. Butcher stood on Grub's shoulders as a tall guest. But as soon as they slipped into the tent, a nobleman stopped to talk to them, "Impeccable weather for these joyous festivities! Are you acquainted with the bride or the groom?"

"The groom, chip chip! A fine young lad! I went to finishing school with his father," Butcher replied in a fake accent. He was so busy talking and looking around that he didn't notice Grub reach out from the costume pants to feel around the buffet table for some food. He had just grabbed a pastry when one of the ladies saw him and screamed. They'd been caught!

Across the tent, Snow White stepped up onto a chair and clinked a fork against a glass as if she was going to make a toast to get the attention of the panicked guests. "This is a stickup!" she announced.

The crowd screamed, yelled, and began to rush toward the exits—but the dwarves had them blocked in. Butcher walked up behind the Prince and clubbed him over the head with a big hammer. The prince fell over, unconscious.

It was pandemonium—just how Snow White wanted it.

Meanwhile, the Queen was getting dressed for her big day. She made a beautiful bride if she did say so herself. She looked young, glowing, and she even fit into her old wedding dress. Well, she didn't fit into it quite yet, but she would before the ceremony if she had anything to say about it. She had an entire team working on it.

Margaret the Baker was doing her best to get the Queen's gown to fasten, but she wasn't having much luck, even with three maids pulling and pushing the fabric into place.

"Further! Harder, harder," the Queen demanded. "I must look glorious today. This is every woman's special day."

"How special can it be? You've been married five times," Margaret asked, out of breath. "It just doesn't fit, Your Highness."

"You must have shrunk it, Baker Lady," the Queen replied.

Just then Brighton came in, his clothing torn and his hair a mess. "I was a cockroach!" he yelled at the Queen. He was shaking and still terrified from his experience. "It was a nightmare! I was crunchy, and small, and I had an exoskeleton. Everybody tried to step on me. I was covered in germs."

The Queen sighed and rolled her eyes at him. "Brighton, this is all very fascinating, but it's my wedding day, and we don't really have time for your petty problems."

"But I was a bug!" Brighton mumbled.

"Just zip me up," the Queen demanded.

Brighton frowned, then begrudgingly helped. The Queen sucked in her stomach. Margaret and several other maids pulled tight and finally the dress zipped up!

"There! See, I knew I was the same size." The Queen spun around in front of the mirror, admiring her reflection. "It's time to get rich. . . . I mean get hitched."

Brighton and Margaret walked the Queen to the tent for the ceremony. Trumpeters outside sounded their horns. The Queen patted her hair and fluffed her bouquet before nodding at Brighton. "Announcing Her Royal Highness, the Queen," Brighton announced.

"No matter how many times I do it, I still get excited on my wedding day," the Queen admitted with a smile.

Brighton pulled open the tent for the Queen's grand entrance. She walked in and down the aisle slowly, but instead of her admiring subjects showering her with compliments, she was greeted with a very strange sight indeed — all of her guests were sitting on the ground in their underwear.

"Oh no," Brighton whispered.

"What is it with this kingdom?" the Queen demanded, throwing her bouquet on the ground and stomping her foot. "You turn your back for five minutes, and it turns into a nudist colony."

The Baron marched over to her, enraged. "This is outrageous. Your Highness, if you are unfit to handle a few bandits, then you're unfit to rule! The Gentry are calling for you to be deposed."

"Baron, did you say 'deposed'?" she hissed.

But the Baron refused to back down. He was tired of the Queen and her games. "Yes, I did, Your Majesty! Deposed, expelled, removed from office . . ."

"Okay, easy, Baron. I know you're cross because I rejected your proposal of marriage," she said pointedly in front of the entire crowd.

The Baron flushed bright red, blustering, "This has nothing to do with that."

"Whatever you say," the Queen answered in a condescending tone. "It's just a little robbery. There will still be a glorious wedding. Someone grab the Prince."

"I'm afraid that's impossible, Your Majesty," Margaret replied.

"Huh? And why is that?" the Queen asked.

"Because the Prince has been kidnapped," Margaret replied, obviously thrilled with the news.

"What? B-by whom?"

"Snow White."

The Queen was enraged. Her eyes narrowed dangerously. "What?" the Queen demanded, then muttered to herself, "I guess if you want someone dead you have to do it yourself."

The Baron seized the opening to address the crowd again. "If this Queen cannot control her own kingdom, then I think we all must decide whether she is fit to rule."

He turned to face her, but the Queen was already gone.

chapter twenty-six

Snow White and the dwarves had managed to get the Prince to the dwarves' cottage, but they hadn't figured out how to break the Queen's spell. They had tied him to a chair to keep him still, but he wouldn't stop crying and begging for the Queen.

"Please take me back to my precious Queen!" the Prince begged. "*Pleeeeeeaase!* I beg you! I yearn for the nectar of her skin."

"Nectar of her skin?" Grub repeated.

"Who talks like that?" Half-Pint wondered.

"It has to be a spell, right?" Grimm asked.

"That sounds like the Queen," Snow answered. "Does anyone know how to break a spell?"

They tried slapping, punching, hitting, pinching, and even throwing water on the Prince. Nothing worked.

"My only pain is the Queen's absence," the Prince moaned.

The dwarves all moaned, too. It was exhausting trying to break a spell.

"Anybody else have any more ideas?" Snow asked. It was starting to look hopeless.

"Oh my!" Napoleon exclaimed suddenly. "I don't know why I didn't think of it before! A kiss! The kiss of true love is always what liberates someone from a spell."

"That's the stupidest thing I've ever heard," Half-Pint replied.

"Oh, and you're just full of great ideas," Napoleon snapped sarcastically.

"It's not how a girl imagines her first kiss. But I guess it's worth a try," Snow said, nodding.

Everyone went quiet. Snow White looked at the Prince. She was nervous and excited and a little afraid. She took a step forward, but suddenly Napoleon shouted, "Wait! If it's the girl's first kiss, we can do better than this! We must do her hair, get her a new dress. This is a big moment!"

The dwarves took Snow into the other room and sat her in a chair. Then Napoleon styled her hair. Grub stuck his finger in strawberry jam and ran it over her lips so they were shiny and red. Wolf straightened her dress and fluffed her skirt. She looked beautiful. Snow smiled at herself in the mirror and then walked over to the Prince.

The Prince watched her coming and realized what was about to happen. He flailed around. "No! Cease this torture!" he demanded, but Snow White just walked closer and closer. Under the spell, he couldn't remember that he loved Snow.

"Shut your eyes. Go slow. Feel the passion. . . ." Napoleon coached from the sidelines.

Snow leaned in to kiss him, then stopped. She turned to the dwarves, "A little privacy, guys?"

The dwarves frowned and then walked out of the room. They hated to miss the big moment, but they understood.

Finally, Snow White bent down so that she was face-to-face with the Prince and whispered, "Come back to me, please." Then she leaned in, untied him, and kissed him tenderly on the lips. It was the perfect kiss.

The Prince's eyes opened slowly, clear and full of love for Snow White. The spell was broken!

The dwarves peeked back around the door one by one, holding their breath. Finally, Snow White pulled away.

The Prince pretended to still be under the spell. He opened his eyes slowly and murmured, "The Queen . . . the Queen . . ."

The dwarves moaned. They had been so sure it would work. Snow turned away from him. Her heart was broken. She could feel tears gathering in her eyes.

". . . is an awful, miserable woman," the Prince finished. "And Snow White is the most magical girl in the world." Snow turned to see the Prince smiling at her. "Gotcha!"

"That whole time, you were out of the spell!" she exclaimed, rushing over to untie him. Snow geared up to scold him, but instead, he scooped her up in his arms and kissed her again.

chapter twenty-seven

The Queen galloped through the forest, pushing her horse as fast as it would go. She was sick of leaving everything up to someone else. She wanted Snow White and those horrible dwarves gone, and she was going to make sure it happened that night.

🍎 🍎 🍎

Snow White and the dwarves were busy planning their next attack and bringing the Prince up to speed with no idea that the Queen was headed their way.

"What do you mean, I was going to marry the Queen? I don't even like the Queen!" The Prince demanded.

"It's true. Look at what you're wearing!" Snow answered

with a giggle. He looked down at his tight, ruffled pink shirt and grimaced. "You even craved . . ."

"The 'nectar of her skin,'" Chuck finished.

"This is utter madness! I thank you from the depths of my heart for saving me!" he smiled, but then became serious. "When I met all of you, I called you 'kiddies' and other cruel names. But I was wrong. You are gallant, and men without equals!"

The dwarves were touched. It meant a lot to them that the Prince appreciated their hard work.

"And you're not the twit we thought you were," Butcher grudgingly admitted.

Grimm elbowed Butcher. "Shut up!" he hissed.

Just then the Beast's loud howl cut through the night. It sounded like it was right outside.

"What's the Beast doing here?" Grimm wondered aloud.

"It never comes to this side of the forest," Grub agreed.

"He's here for me," Snow announced quietly. She had been expecting the Queen to strike back and she had always wondered if the Queen and the Beast were linked. After all, the Beast arrived in the woods around the same time her father married the Queen. "Gentlemen, I can think of no greater group of warriors to lead into battle than those who stand before me right now." She held out her gold dagger and raised it high. "But this is my fight."

Then Snow White turned, ran out the door, and locked it from the outside. She couldn't let the Prince or her friends get hurt for her.

Inside, the dwarves hammered on the door.

"Snow!" Half-Pint yelled. "Stop!"

"You'll die!" Napoleon added.

"You can't beat the Beast alone!" Grimm hollered.

The Prince threw himself against the door hard.

Snow White turned and spoke loudly through the door, "You know, all that time stuck in the castle, I did a lot of reading. I read so many stories where the Prince saves the Princess in the end. I think it's time we change the ending."

"Snow! Wait!" the Prince called. He put his palm against the door. On the outside, Snow put her palm against the door, too.

"It was a perfect first kiss," she said.

"Snow!" he cried. But with that, she turned and ran into the forest toward the howls from the Beast. She needed to face the Beast on her own, once and for all.

🍎 🍎 🍎

"If you're looking for me, I'm right here," Snow yelled, running into a clearing.

The Queen stood alone in the clearing, rubbing her half-moon pendant thoughtfully.

"You! What are you doing here?" Snow demanded. She had been expecting the Beast. The Queen didn't usually do her own dirty work.

"Oh, just taking a stroll, clearing my head. I don't know if you heard but . . ." The Queen leaned forward and whispered conspiratorially, "My wedding got robbed."

The Beast brayed close by, interrupting. The trees on the edge of the clearing rustled and swayed. He was about to break through. Snow White gripped her dagger more tightly, holding it in front of her, ready to strike. But then the Queen simply touched her pendant and raised her hand in a stop motion. The Beast stopped in his tracks on the edge of the clearing. Snow White could just make out his grotesque shape in the shadows.

"There, there, hold on now. Who's my good boy? You are, aren't you?" the Queen cooed at the waiting Beast. He moaned and whined, eager to get to Snow. "Yes you are! You're my scary people-killing beast. Aren't you? Aren't you?"

Snow White glared at the Queen. She knew something had been fishy about the Beast. "The Beast doesn't frighten you?" Snow asked to confirm her hunch.

"The Beast? No, of course not," the Queen answered honestly, all deception gone. "*You* frighten me, Snow White. I'll admit it now only because you're about to die. But you truly frighten me. I knew what you were from the first moment I looked into your eyes. *You* are my beast. You are more beautiful than me—younger, sweeter, the fairest in all the land. And you are the only person who can take everything from me."

The Beast brayed loudly, his snout peeking out from the leaves.

"Him?" she continued, "He's my sweet little avenger. Does whatever I command him. He slaughtered the villagers. He slaughtered the Prince's valet. And now, he's going to slaughter you."

"Is my father not worthy of being mentioned?" Snow asked, stricken.

"Sure, put him on the list, why not? Don't say I never did anything for you."

"I am made of more than you think, you know," Snow replied, drawing herself up to her full height and looking the Queen right in the eyes.

The Queen laughed contemptuously. "Yeah, well okay." Then she turned toward the Beast, dropped her hand, and ordered, "Kill her."

The Beast charged out of the trees right at Snow White, while the Queen laughed. She didn't need to stay and watch. It was finally over. She strode out of the clearing, climbed onto her horse, and rode back to the castle, smiling to herself the entire time. "Die well, Snow White."

Back at the house, the Prince and the dwarves refused to give up. They knew they had to help Snow. They took turns pounding on the door. Finally, the Prince lost his temper.

"Move!" he demanded. He stepped back and kicked at the door with all of his might until he was out of breath. He looked at the dwarves and shrugged. "Please send my compliments to your carpenter. That is one tough door. No one has a key?"

Grub cleared his throat and sheepishly pulled a key strung on a chain around his neck. He hadn't even thought of unlocking it. The dwarves all groaned. The Prince snatched the key, ran to the door, then turned back to them, "It's been a long time coming, gentlemen, but I think I've finally found something worth fighting for."

The dwarves cheered, heading after him. But then, with a smile, the Prince rushed out the door and locked it behind him.

"Not again!" Grimm exclaimed, hammering on the door.

"Why do we keep getting locked in our own house?" Half-Pint demanded.

chapter
twenty-eight

Getting out of the house a second time wasn't as easy, but the dwarves finally found a way to use their biggest strength—their short stature! Wolf climbed out of the tiny second-story window, slid down the slanted roof, and landed in front of the door.

"Owww oww owwwwwwwww!" Wolf howled as he opened the door and let his friends out.

The dwarves charged out into the forest, ready for battle! They rushed through the forest and followed the howls and shrieks of the Beast to find Snow and the Prince.

Snow White ran through the woods, the Beast close behind, until she reached a dead end. There was nowhere else for her to go. It was time to fight. Gasping for breath, she turned and bumped right into—the Prince!

"Ahhhh!" she shrieked. "What are you doing here?"

"If I die, I die beside the woman I love," he said, reaching out to hold her hand.

"If I wasn't about to fight a vicious beast, I'd surely kiss you," Snow replied.

"If I wasn't about to fight it, too, I'd surely let you." They smiled at each other, but the Prince's smiled dropped as he saw the Beast barreling out of the trees behind Snow White. The Prince pushed Snow out of his way and fearlessly engaged the Beast. Snow spun around him and fought, too. They slashed at the Beast shoulder to shoulder, a true team.

The Beast struck at Snow and sent her flying into a tree. She dropped her dagger and fell to the ground, dazed. The Prince turned so that he was in front of her, protecting her while she recovered.

The Prince hacked away at the Beast, but the Beast was so fast. It kept pushing forward, gaining on the Prince, when suddenly the Beast turned his head and shrieked. Rocks were raining down on his head! The dwarves had arrived and were pelting it with rocks.

"If it's your fight, it's our fight," Butcher announced to Snow White.

The Beast grunted and then stomped the ground and pounded the dirt with its tail. The ground shook and the dwarves tumbled to the ground like dominoes. The Prince took advantage of the Beast's distraction and rushed forward, his sword aimed at its throat, but the Beast whipped around at the last moment. It stuck its tail out and grabbed the Prince with it, thrashing him around like a rag doll before pinning him against a thick tree. The Prince squirmed and twisted but couldn't break free.

Snow watched in horror as her friends fell. She had to pull herself together. She stood up, shaking off her injuries, but she couldn't find her dagger. She dropped to the ground again, feeling around for the gold weapon in the shadows.

The Beast lumbered toward her, relishing the moment.

"No!" Grimm shouted. They couldn't let the Beast get her.

"I've got it!" Napoleon yelled. He had spotted a glint in the bushes nearby—it was Snow's golden dagger. He grabbed it, tossed it to Chuck, who tossed it to Half-Pint, who tossed it to the Prince. The Prince struggled and finally wrenched one arm free and caught it at the last moment.

"Snow!" the Prince yelled and then tossed the dagger to Snow. She reached up and snatched it out of the air and then

131

whipped around to face the Beast, who was right behind her.

The Beast opened his mouth, revealing rows of jagged, razor-sharp teeth coated with slimy spit. Snow was trembling with fear, her dagger shaking in her hand. Then Snow saw something odd—buried deep in the Beast's furry neck hung a tarnished half-moon pendant. It was the same pendant that the Queen had given to Snow's father so many years ago. She gasped—it couldn't be, could it?

"Kill it!" The Prince yelled.

"You've got him!" Napoleon agreed.

"Just do it!" Grub hollered.

The Beast growled and moved closer. But Snow White looked up from the pendant and into the Beast's eyes and into its soul. Something in those eyes was so familiar. Snow only had a moment to act, so she had to make a choice. She reached out swiftly with her dagger and cut the cord on the pendant. The shining half-moon fell to the ground with a dull thud and cracked on a sharp rock.

Back in the palace, the Queen was relishing her victory and gloating to the Mirror Queen when her half-moon pendant suddenly fell from her neck and shattered on the floor.

The Queen looked down, her mouth hanging open. It

couldn't be! She looked up at the Mirror Queen sharply.

"You ready to discover the price of using magic?" the Mirror Queen asked with a cruel smile.

"No. No. Noooo!" the Queen wailed as a bright light burst from the broken pendant and enveloped her. Everywhere the light touched her, she aged rapidly. Her hands shriveled and age spots bloomed on her pale skin. Her face crumpled, wrinkles etching themselves over her forehead, cheeks, and skin. The skin on her neck drooped, hanging loosely off of her thin frame. Her shoulders bowed and her spine bent as she became hunched and drawn. She would never be the fairest in the land again. She was hideous.

The Mirror Queen laughed a high, evil laugh as the light faded away and the Queen's crown dropped on to the ground and spun like a coin in circles until it finally settled with a resounding clang on the hard, cold floor.

A bright light burst from the broken pendant and enveloped the Beast. The Beast transformed before Snow White's eyes. Its scales and claws and dragonlike face shrunk and morphed, glowing brighter and brighter until there was a dazzling explosion. When the smoke cleared, the King, Snow White's father, stood before her, dazed and confused.

"Father?" Snow White whispered with tears in her eyes. It was too good to be true.

"Snow?" he asked, studying the beautiful young woman before him. His daughter was a grown woman—what had happened to him? He opened his arms and Snow rushed into them.

"You're alive. I can't believe it, you're alive!" she exclaimed. "I thought you were gone forever."

The King pulled back, holding her at arm's length so he could take her in. He reached out and wiped the tears from her cheek and reached up to stroke her hair. "You're all grown-up! But I don't understand . . . you were just a child . . ."

"I know. It's a really long story," she said, the pain of those years clear in her eyes.

He thought hard, trying to remember, and it finally dawned on him—it had to have been the Queen. "The Queen? This was her doing?" Snow nodded. "Forgive me," he continued, near tears himself. "I thought I wasn't enough."

"You were always enough for me."

The King pulled his daughter in close for another hug. They were both overwhelmed by all that had happened, how many years they had lost, and what they had just gained.

The Prince and the dwarves edged forward cautiously. The King and Snow finally broke their hug and the King slowly turned to the Prince. "And who are these young men?" he asked his daughter.

The Prince knelt in front of the King.

"This is the Prince of Valencia. He risked his life to save our kingdom," Snow announced and then gestured to the dwarves standing behind the Prince, "and his most valiant soldiers."

The dwarves all bowed to their King.

"That's very generous of you, Princess, but you took care of matters quite well on your own," the Prince replied.

The King chuckled. He knew a spark when he saw it. "Nonetheless, for your bravery, we will forever be in your debt. Is there any way I can repay you?"

"Gold!" Butcher shouted.

"A feast!" Grub added.

"There is only one thing I desire, Your Majesty," the Prince said humbly. Then he looked over at Snow White and smiled eagerly.

chapter twenty-nine

Princess Snow White and the Prince of Valencia's wedding couldn't have been more different than the Queen's failed wedding attempt. Everyone from the village was in attendance for the sweet ceremony and simple feast and the spoiled lords and ladies were nowhere in sight.

Snow looked radiant in a beautiful blue gown and her crown, and the Prince was every inch the dashing prince in his finest regalia. The dwarves lined up behind the Prince as his groomsmen, in formal suits with shining gold medals from the King around their necks. The couple stood in front of the King and everyone in the room could see how in love they were.

"Among the privileges afforded a King, there is none greater than the power to join two people together in matrimony," the King said, turning to the Prince, "My son, you found this kingdom caught in the clutches of greed and vanity. But rather than retreat, you heroically entered the fight, displaying a level of heroism well beyond your years. We all owe you—and your brave compatriots: Grimm, Grub, Half-Pint, Napoleon, Wolf, Butcher, and Chuck—a great debt of gratitude." Then the King turned to his daughter. "Snow White, my daughter . . . this kingdom was fortunate, for in my absence, you never stopped believing in yourself, and grew into the woman I'd always hoped you'd become. Despite impossible odds, you faced the Queen and defeated her, forever ridding this land of her wretched ways."

The Prince's family and all of the townspeople cheered loudly. Snow smiled at her father, tears in her eyes. She felt so good that she had made her father and her kingdom proud.

"As our new Queen, I know you will lead the people—all of the people—big, small, rich, and poor—with kindness and compassion, because your beauty shines most brightly from within your heart. Therefore, as my final act as King—and by the power vested in me by, well, me—I now pronounce you husband and wife. You may kiss the bride."

The Prince and Snow smiled shyly at each other. Then the Prince stepped forward and spun Snow White into a perfect dip, kissing her passionately.

The crowd cheered loudly, tossing confetti and streamers into the air.

Snow and the Prince took time at their reception to greet every guest. The villagers were eager to meet their new Queen and King and give them simple gifts as thanks for saving them from the evil Queen.

Snow hugged and kissed all of the children and listened as each person told her their names and what they did. She had a lot to do to help her people and she wanted to know each of her subjects. When a very frail old woman walked up, Snow reached out to hold her hand.

"It would warm my ancient heart if you would accept this modest gift on your wedding day," the woman said in a quavering voice. She reached into her pocket and pulled out a very red, shiny apple.

"How dear of you," Snow replied sweetly, taking the apple. Snow was about to take a bite when she looked into the old woman's eyes.

"Just one bite . . ." the woman coaxed, but the voice sounded familiar all of a sudden. ". . . for good fortune."

Snow White shined the apple on her skirt and spoke quietly,

but firmly, "Someone once told me: A great leader can look a person in the eye and know exactly what they are." Snow knew with one look in the old woman's eyes that the old woman was actually the evil Queen, and she wasn't about to let her get away. Snow pulled her golden dagger from her pocket and cut a slice from the apple. She held the slice out to the old queen generously, "Age before beauty."

The old queen froze, looking around for a way out. But the dwarves stood around her in a loose circle. There was no escape.

"It's important to know when you've been beaten," Snow continued, throwing the Queen's words back at her.

The old woman bowed her head. Snow White had won in the end. She took the apple slice and held it up to her shriveled lips. "At least I'm not going by myself," she said.

Inside the magical mirror, the Mirror Queen shivered with fear. "No. No! NOOOOOOOOOOOOOOOOOO!" she shrieked as all of the glass in the magical cottage exploded one piece at a time, shards flying everywhere.

Finally, the Mirror Queen exploded into a million pieces of glass. The Mirror Queen's screams faded away and all that was left was the soft tinkle of glass hitting the floor.

The Mirror Queen and the evil Queen were both gone for good.

With that, the kingdom erupted in cheers. Snow had rid evil from their land and they could finally live in peace and happiness. Snow smiled at the Prince and knew that everything would be happiness from that day forward.

epilogue

I t was a perfect summer day with the sun shining and birds singing until the sounds of swords crossing shattered the peaceful air.

"En garde!" the Prince yelled. He whipped around, swinging his sword until it hit against Snow White's.

"Is this really necessary?" Snow asked, lazily blocking his blow.

"I deserve a rematch, a chance to erase the defeat from my memory. And I warn you—this time I won't go easy on you."

"Easy?" Snow White demanded. Insulted, she held up her hand so he would pause. She took off her crown, the crown of a true queen, and set it aside. Then she rolled up her sleeves and held up her sword. She was ready to fight.

"Surely, you know I allowed you to beat me last time," her husband continued.

Snow raised an eyebrow skeptically. "It's not often that a man allows a woman to beat him unconscious."

"I was attempting to bolster your self-esteem."

"How very sweet of you."

"This time, it's just us. *Mano a mano.*"

"I think you mean, *mano e lado*," she laughed, enjoying their flirtatious banter as they circled each other, preparing to spar. "I am a lady, after all."

"Indeed you are. The most beautiful one in the land."

"Flattery will get you nowhere. I'm still gonna kick your butt."

The Prince smiled the same way that had captured Snow White's heart the first time they met.

"Why do you have to be so cute?" she asked, and with that she lunged at him, laughing with pure joy.

And they lived happily ever after.